THE BURNING

The Iowa School of Letters Award for Short Fiction

THE BURNING

&
OTHER
STORIES

Jack Cady

UNIVERSITY OF IOWA PRESS
IOWA CITY

for Patricia of Arlington

CONTENTS

The Burning   13

The Girl in the Orange Hat   25

The Forest Ranger   35

I Take Care of Things   45

Land   53

Text and Notes . . .   57

Play Like I'm Sheriff   65

The Shark   77

The Sounds of Silence   85

The Art of a Lady   95

Ride the Thunder   107

The Troll   119

Thermopylae   129

With No Breeze   137

PREFACE

What does this writer see? How does he see it? Does he project his vision with enough skill to let you into his world and keep you there? How full and complete is the experience he gives us? These are questions one always asks when picking up a new writer's book for the first time. Jack Cady gives us a rich variety of experiences and characters: truck drivers with troubled consciences over the death of a fellow truck driver on the road, an artist in San Francisco getting to know what his wife is really like through her response to a girl in an orange hat, a father taking his son north to Canada to escape the draft, a man and a woman meeting casually in a city and managing to transcend their loneliness for an evening, playing like they were somebodies to each other.

I read Cady's manuscript through completely the first time. He has a tough-minded vision of things, but a compassionate and mature one. His people think and feel deeply about themselves and their relationships with each other. They don't deny experience or retreat from it; when things happen to them they try to come to terms with the experience as best they can. They carry the burden of their lives with a courage reminiscent of Hemingway characters, though Cady's people lead quieter lives.

Cady projects his vision in a direct, unpretentious style; the stories are quiet, and achieve themselves in a ruthless and tense precision. Not a wasted moment here. And much pleasure to be discovered.

William M. Murray
Iowa City, 1972

JACK CADY

Jack Cady was born in Columbus, Ohio, in 1932. He has travelled extensively in North America and Europe, and has lived on both the East and West Coasts, as well as in the Middle West. Cady has taught writing and American literature at the University of Washington in Seattle since 1968. His prizes include the Atlantic Monthly First Award for 1965, the American Literary Anthology Award for 1970, and the 1972 Iowa School of Letters Award for Short Fiction. He believes that the duty of a writer is "to portray with complete accuracy the visible and invisible worlds of his perception."

The Burning

S UNLIGHT gleamed as Singleton and I walked down the hill to the charred wreckage of what had been a truck. Gates was dead, and the breeze lifted sooty material that mixed with the valley smells of weeds, flowers, and diesel stink. Manny was in jail. Nothing more could be done for Gates, but now Manny was sitting in his own fire, burning because he was kind, because he was gentle.

Traffic was moving as usual on the long slopes; only an occasional car slowed, its occupants looking over the scene of last night's fire. The truck drivers would know all about the trouble, and they did not want to see. Besides, there was a hill to climb on either side of the valley. They could not afford to lose speed. I knew that by now the word of the burning had spread at least a hundred miles. As far as Lexington, drivers would be leaning against counters listening, with wildness spreading in them. Singleton and I had not slept through the long night. We revisited the scene because we felt it was the final thing we could do for both men.

Close up the sunlight played on bright runs of metal where someone had pulled the cab apart hoping to recover enough of Gates's remains for burial. An oil fire, when the oil is pouring on a man, doesn't leave much. Only the frame and other heavy structural members of the truck remained.

"If he had only been knocked out or killed before the fire got to him . . . ." We were both thinking the words. Either might have said them.

"His company's sending an investigator," Singleton told me. "But since we're here, let's go over it. They'll be sure to ask."

"Are you going to pull?"

"No." He shook his head and ran his hand across his face. "No. Next week maybe or the week after. I'm not steady. I called for three drivers. That's one for your rig too."

"Thanks. I've got vacation coming. I'm taking it."

The road surface along the wreck was blackened, and the asphalt waved and sagged. It was a bad spot. The state should have put up signs. Forty-seven feet of power and payload; now it seemed little there in the ditch, its unimportance turning my stomach. I wanted to retch. I felt lonely and useless.

We walked to the far hill to look at the tire marks. Narrow little lines which swung wide across the other lane and then back in, suddenly breaking and spinning up the roadway. Heavy black lines were laid beside them where the driver of the car being passed had ridden his brakes and then gone on up the hill. Coming down were the marks Gates made, and they showed that he had done what a trucker is supposed to do. He had avoided at all costs. The marks ran off the road.

I never knew him. Manny, tall, sandy-haired, and laughing, was my good friend, but I did not know Gates. I did not know until later that Singleton knew him.

We had picked Gates up twenty miles back on the narrow two-lane that ran through the Kentucky hills. We rode behind him figuring to pass when he got a chance to let us around. It was early, around 3 A.M., but there was still heavy vacation-season traffic. Manny was out front behind Gates. My rig was second behind him, and Singleton was behind me. Our three freights were grossing less than fifty thousand so we could go.

Gates's tanker must have scaled at around sixty thousand. Even with that weight you can usually go, but his gas-powered tractor was too light.

It slowed us to be laying back, but there was no reason to dog it. He was making the best time he could. He topped the hill by June's Stop and ran fast after he crested on the long slope down. He had Manny by maybe two hundred yards because Manny had signaled into June's.

When he signaled I checked my mirrors. Singleton kept pulling so I kept pulling. When he saw us coming on, Manny canceled the signal and went over the top behind Gates. It allowed enough of a lag for Gates to get out front, and it kept Manny from being killed.

We took the hill fast. You have to climb out the other side. I was a quarter mile back, running at forty-five and gaining speed, when I saw the headlights of the little car swing into the lane ahead of Gates's tanker. The driver had incorrectly estimated the truck's speed or the car's passing power.

It was quick and not bad at first. The tanker went into the ditch. The car cut back in, broke traction, and spun directly up the roadway. It came to a stop next to Manny's rig, almost brushing against his drive axle and not even bending sheet metal, a fluke. The car it had passed went onto the shoulder and recovered. The driver took it on up the hill to get away from the wreck and involvement.

Manny was closer. He had perhaps a second more to anticipate the wreck. He had stopped quicker than I believed possible. It was about a minute before the fire started. I was running with my extinguisher when I saw it, and knew I would be too late.

"I wish he'd exploded," Singleton said. He kicked up dust along the roadway. He was too old for this, and he was beat-out and shaken. The calmness of resignation was trying to take him, and I hoped it would. I wondered to myself if those clear eyes that had looked down a million and a half miles of road had ever looked at anything like this.

"Exploded? Yes, either that or got out."

"He was hurt. I think he was hurt bad." He looked at me almost helplessly. "No sense wishing; let's go back up. "

After the wreck Singleton had backed his rig over the narrow two-lane, following the gradual bend of the road in the dark. He had taken the two girls from the small car into his cab.

I had stayed a little longer until Gates's burning got really bad. Then I brought the little car in, feeling the way I feel in any car: naked, unprotected, and nearly blind. I was shaking from weakness. The road was blocked above. There was no oncoming beyond the pot flares. The cop with the flashlight had arrived ten or fifteen minutes after the wreck. Behind me the fire rose against the summer blackness and blanketed the valley with the acrid smell of number-two diesel. Because of the distance, Manny's rig seemed almost in the middle of the fire and silhouetted against the burning, though I knew he had stopped nearly fifty yards up the roadway. My own rig was pulled in behind him; its markers stood pale beside the bigger glow. As I was about to go past the cop, he waved me over.

"Where you taking it?"

"Just to the top," I told him. "The girls were pretty shaken up. Don't worry, they won't go anywhere."

"Think they need an ambulance?" He paused, uncertain. "Christ," he said. "Will that other cruiser ever get here?"

"What about Manny?" I asked.

"In there." He nodded to where Manny sat in the cruiser. The lights were out inside. He could not be seen. "I'll take a statement at the top. You'll see him at the top."

I wanted to call to Manny, but there was nothing I could do. I took the car on to June's Stop. Rigs were starting to pile in, even stacking up along the roadway. Cars were parked around and between them, blacked out and gleaming small and dull in the lights from the truck markers. Most of the guys had cut their engines. It would be a long wait.

Singleton's truck was down by the restaurant. Inside around the counter, which formed a kind of box, drivers were sitting and talking. A few were standing around. They were excited and walked back and forth. I wanted coffee, needed it, but I could not go in. At least not then. A driver came up behind me.

"You Wakefield?" he asked. He meant did I drive for Wake-field. My name is Arnold.

I told him yes.

"Your buddy took the girls to Number Twelve. He said to come."

"As if we didn't have enough trouble . . . ."

"He's got the door open." The guy grinned. He was short with a light build and was in too good a mood. I disliked him right away.

"Listen," he said. "They say there's going to be a shakedown."

"Who says?"

"Who knows? That's just the word. If you left anything back there, you'd better get it out. Check it with June."

He meant guns and pills. A lot of companies require them in spite of the law. A lot of guys carry them on their own, the guns I mean. Pills are Benzedrine, Bennies, or a stronger kind called footballs. Only drivers who don't know any better use them to stay awake or get high on.

"I've got it right here," I told him, and patted my side pocket. "I'll hang onto it myself."

"Your funeral," he said, grinning. He gave me a sick feeling. He was a guy with nose trouble, one who spreads his manure up and down the road, a show-off to impress waitresses. "Thanks," I said, and turned to go to the motel room.

"Hey," he yelled, "what do you think will happen to him?"

"You figure it out." I went over to the motel, found Twelve, and went inside.

The room had twin beds. Singleton was sitting on one, facing the two girls on the other. One was kind of curled up. The other was leaning forward still crying. Vassar, I thought. No, nothing like that on 25 South; University of Kentucky likely, but the same sorry type. I edged down beside Singleton. "Why do you bother?" I asked him. "To hell with them." The girl bawling looked up hard for a moment and started bawling worse.

"I had room," she bawled.

We were all under a strain. The diesel smell was bad, but the other smell that I would never forget had been worse. Even away from the fire I seemed still to smell it.

"You thought you had room!" I yelled at her.

"No, really. I was all right. I had room." She was convinced, almost righteous. At some other time she might have been pretty. Both were twenty or twenty-one. The curled-up one was sort of mousy-looking. The one who was bawling was tall with long hair. I thought of her as a thing.

"No—really," I yelled at her; "you had no room, but keep lying to yourself. Pretty soon that'll make everything OK."

"Leave it, Arn," Singleton told me. "You're not doing any good."

He went to the sink to wet a towel, bringing it to the girl. "Wipe your face," he told her. Then he turned to me. "Did you bring their car?"

"I brought it—just a minute. You can have them in just a minute." I was still blind angry. "Old, young, men, women, we've seen too many of their kind. I just want to say it once." I looked directly at her. "How much have you driven?"

For a moment it didn't take; then she understood.

"Five years."

"Not years. Miles."

"Why—I guess—I don't know. Five years."

"Five thousand a year? Ten thousand? That would be plenty; you haven't driven that much. Five years times ten is fifty thousand. That's six to eight months' work for those guys down there. You *had no room!*" I bit it out at her. She just looked confused, and I felt weak. "I'm ready to leave it now," I told Singleton. "I should have known. Remember, we've got a friend down there."

"I've got two."

He looked different than ever before. He sat slouched on the bed and leaned forward a little. His hands were in his lap, and the lines and creases in his face were shadowed in the half-light from the floor lamp.

"Who was he?" I asked.

He looked at me. I realized with a shock that he had been fighting back tears, but his eyes were gray and clear as always. The silver hair that had been crossed with dark streaks as long as I had known him now seemed a dull gray. The hands in his lap were steady. He reached into a pocket.

"Get coffee." He looked at the girls. "Get two apiece for everybody."

"Who was it, Singleton?"

"Get the coffee. We'll talk later." He looked at the girl who was curled up. "She's not good."

"Shock?"

"Real light. If it was going to get worse, I think it would have. Maybe you'd better bring June." He got up again and tried to straighten the curled-up girl. He asked her to turn on her back. She looked OK. She tried to fight him. "Help him," I told the one who had been bawling.

The restaurant was better than a hundred yards off. A hillbilly voice was deviling a truck song. June was in the kitchen, I told her I needed help, and she came right away. Business is one thing, people are another. She has always been that way. She brought a Silex with her, and we walked back across the lot. In the distance there was the sound of two sirens crossing against each other.

"The other police car."

"That and a fire truck," she told me.

June is a fine woman, once very pretty but now careless of her appearance and too heavy. It is always sad and a little strange to see a nice-looking woman allow herself to slide. There must be reasons, but not the kind that bear thinking about. She had a good hand with people, a good way. She ran a straight business. When we came to the room, she asked us to leave and started mothering the girls. We went outside with the coffee and sat on the step.

"I'm sorry," I told him. "I shouldn't have blown up, but for a minute I could have killed them. I hate every fool like them."

"It's their road too."

"I know."

"Everybody makes mistakes. You—me—nobody has perfect judgment."

"But not like that."

"No. No, we're not like that, but she won't ever be again either. She has to live with that."

I understood a little more about him. He was good in his judgment. It was suddenly not a matter for us to forgive. There was the law. It had nothing to do with us.

"Manny never held those brakes against you," he told me.

Once I had checked his truck for him, and he had a failure. I wanted to say that it was different.

We sat listening to the muffled sounds from the room behind us. Soon, off at the downhill corner of the lot, headlights appeared coming from the wreck. The state car cruised across the lot. It stopped at the end of the motel row. Singleton stood up and motioned to him. The car moved toward us, rolling in gently. The cop got out. Manny was sitting in the back seat. He was slumped over and quiet. When the cop slammed the door, he did not look up.

He was an older cop, too old to be riding a cruiser. In the darkness and excitement there had been no way to tell much about him. He was tired and walked to us unofficially. We made room for him on the step. He sat between us, letdown, his hands shaking with either fatigue or nervousness.

"Charles," he said to Singleton, "who was he?"

"You'd better have some coffee," Singleton told him. He reached over and put his hand on the cop's shoulder. I poured coffee from the Silex, and he drank it fast.

"Gates," said Singleton. "Island Oil. When Haber went broke, I pulled tanks for two years." He stopped as if reflecting. "He was pretty good. I broke him in."

The cop pointed to the car. "Him?"

"Manley, Johnny Manley."

"You're taking him in," I said. "What's the charge?"

"I don't know," the cop told me. "I wouldn't even know what would stick. His rig's half out in one lane. If you're going to say I need a charge, then I'll take him in for obstructing the road."

"I didn't mean that. I'm not trying to push you. I just wanted to see how you felt."

"Then ask straight out. I don't know what I think myself till I get the whole story."

Singleton walked to the car. He leaned through the window to call softly to Manny. Manny did not move, and Singleton leaned against the car for a little while as the cop and I sat and watched. A couple of drivers came by, curious but respectfully silent, and the cop ran them off. June came out with a chair and sat beside the steps. The two girls came out and stood quietly. I looked at them. They were both young, pretty, and in the present circumstances useless and destructively ignorant. I could no longer hate them.

"Is that him?" one of them whispered.

"Yes." I felt like whispering myself. It seemed wrong to be talking about him when he was no more than ten yards off, but I doubted that he was listening to anyone. He was looking down, his long body slumped forward and his hair astray. His face, which was never very good-looking, was drawn tight around his fixed eyes, and his hands were not visible. Perhaps he held them in his lap.

"They can't prove nothing," the cop said. "I bet he gets off." He stood up. "Let's get it over with; we've wasted time."

Singleton came back then. "Tell me," the cop said to him.

"He won't be driving again. I don't know what the law will do, but I know what Manny can't do. He won't take another one out. You can take her statement on the accident"—he pointed at one of the girls—"and his"—he pointed at me. "I was just over the crest—couldn't see it very well. What I can tell you about is afterward, but"—he turned to the girls—"I want to tell you something first because maybe you ought to know. I've known that man yonder seven, eight years. He's a quiet guy. Doesn't say much; really not hard to get to know. He likes people, has patience with them. Sometimes you think he'd be more sociable if he just knew how to start." He hesitated as if searching for words.

"I don't know exactly how to tell it. Instead of talking, he does nice things. Always has extra equipment to spare if the scales are open and the ICC's checking, or maybe puts a bag of apples in your cab before you leave out. Kid stuff—yes, that's it, kid stuff a lot of the time. Sometimes guys don't understand and joke him.

"When he finally got married, it was to a girl who started the whole thing, not him. She was wild. Silly, you know, not especially bad but not the best either. She worked at a stop in Tennessee and quit work after she married instead of going back like she planned. The guy has something. He did good for that girl. I don't know what's going to happen to them now, and it's none of our business I guess, but I just thought you ought to know."

He turned back to the cop. "I came over the crest and saw Manny's and Arnie's stoplights and saw Arnie's trailer jump and pitch sideways till he corrected and got it stopped. I pulled in behind them, and they were both already out and running. Before I got there, I saw the fire. He could tell you more about how it started." He looked at me. I was thinking about it. I nodded for him to go on because it was very real to me, still happening. I wondered if maybe I could get out of having to describe it. I knew there would have to be a corroborative statement, so as Singleton told it I thought along with him.

He did a good job of the telling. He had gotten there only a minute or so after Manny and I were on the scene. Manny jumped from his cab, dodged around the car with the girls in it, and ran to the wreck. I took only enough time to grab my extinguisher. When I got there, Manny was on top of the wreck trying to pull Gates out and holding the door up at the same time.

The tanker had gone in hitting the ditch fast but stretching out the way you want to try to hit a ditch. It had made no motion to jack-knife. The ditch had been too deep, and instead it had lain over on its side. All along there—for that matter, all through those hills—the roadside is usually an outcropping of limestone, slate, and coal. In the cuts and even in the valleys there is rock. Until the truck was pulled off, there would be no way to know. It was likely that the tank and maybe his saddle tank had been opened up on an outcrop of rock. There was a little flicker of fire forward of the cab. Gasoline, I had thought, but it did not grow quick like gasoline. The diesel from his tank was running down the ditch and muffled it some at first.

I went for it with the extinguisher, but it was growing and the extinguisher was a popgun. Manny started yelling to come help him, and I whirled and climbed up over the jutting wheel. Singleton was suddenly there, grabbing me, boosting me up. I took the cab door and held it up, and Gates started to yell.

Manny had him under the shoulders pulling hard, had him about halfway out, but he was hung up. I believe Gates's leg was pinched or held by the wheel. Otherwise Manny would not have gotten him out that far. Manny knew though. He knelt down beside him staring into the wrecked cab.

The fire was getting big behind me, building with a roar. It was flowing down the ditch but gaining backward over the surface rapidly. I gave Manny a little shove and closed the door over Gates's head so we could both reach him through the window. He was a small chunky man—hard to grasp. We got him under the arms and pulled hard, and he screamed again. The heat was close now. I was terrified, confused. We could not pull harder. There was no way to get him out.

Then I was suddenly alone. Manny jumped down, stumbling against Singleton, who tried to climb up and was driven back, his face lined and desperate in the fire glow. Manny disappeared running into the darkness. Where I was above the cab, the air was getting unbearably hot. The fire had not yet worked in under the wreck. I tugged hopelessly until I could no longer bear the heat and jumped down and rolled away. Singleton helped me up and pulled me back just as screams changed from hurt to fear; high weeping, desperate and unbelieving cries as the heat but not the fire got to him.

I was held in horrified disbelief of what was happening. Outside the cab and in front of it were heavy oil flames. Gates, his head and neck and one hand outside the window, was leaning back away from them, screaming another kind of cry because the fire that had been getting close had arrived. The muscles of his neck and face were cast bronze in the fire glow, and his mouth was a wide black circle issuing cries. His eyes were closed tight, and his straining hand tried to pull himself away.

Then there was a noise, and he fell back and disappeared into the fire, quietly sinking to cremation with no further sound, and we turned to look behind us. Manny was standing helplessly, his pistol dropping from his shaking hand to the ground, and then he too was falling to the ground, covering his eyes with his hands and rolling on his side away from us.

"If I'd known, I wouldn't have stopped him," Singleton told the cop. "Of all the men I know, he's the only one who could have done that much."

He hesitated, running his hand through his graying hair. "I didn't help, you understand—didn't help." He looked pleading. "Nothing I could do, no use—Arn didn't help. Only Manny."

The girls and June were sobbing. The sky to the eastward was coming alive with light. The cop who was too old to be riding a cruiser looked blanched and even older in the beginning dawn. I felt as I had once felt at sea after battling an all-night storm. Only Singleton seemed capable of further speech, his almost ancient features passive but alive.

He looked at the patrol car where Manny still slumped. "They can't prove he killed a man. There's nothing to prove it with. They can't even prove the bullet didn't miss, and in a way that's the worst thing that can happen. You see, I know him. You think maybe he'll change after a while—maybe it will dull down and let him live normal. It won't. I sat with him before you came and did what I could, and it was nothing. Do they electrocute in this state or use gas? If they were kind, the way he is kind, they'd do one or the other."

The Girl in the Orange Hat

In San Francisco's Golden Gate Park there is an outdoor amphitheatre where a band plays every Sunday in fine weather. My wife and I always attend the concert.

It is a good place. The program is a mixture of classical, folk, show tunes and pop. It does not require great commitment from the listener, serving me as a leisure time before the inanities of the coming week at the gallery. There I will sell noisy art to noisy people, and only occasionally put a dearly bought painting in the hands of someone who respects the work.

A good place. Sea gulls make slanting wheels in the air, squawking and white against a flat and unfathomable blue. There is sound and color; the band, people's chatter, and occasional individual performances on sitar, guitar or flute. Street people come wearing tiny brass bells, beads and round eye glasses. They tinkle past.

The bandmen's uniforms are black with gold trim and their instruments are gold. The band shell is washed gray concrete. It is framed by the silver and green eucalyptus which rise more than two hundred feet to intercept the wheeling gulls. A concession sells popcorn and hotdogs. There is a picnic smell. It is a large city's aspiration to our memories of small-town bandstands and Saturday nights.

My wife and I bring a blanket to sit on the lawn near one of the high-splashing fountains. Except on very hot days it is a sensual pleasure to be warmed by direct sunlight. We watch each other. At thirty (eight years younger than I) my wife is both beautiful and beautifully proportioned. I can imagine her living in some antique time, sacrificing flowers to Mayan gods. When she dozes on the blanket I sometimes sketch her. Children gather and often wake her with cries:

"Hey, neat!"

"Hey, mister. Draw my dog."

The rest of the people are more sophisticated. They do not trouble us. When my wife wakes it is never to loss. We watch the diversity of people who pass. My wife is a poet. You would easily recognize her name. She is a watcher, a creator whose need to express sometimes confounds me. There is a troubling undercurrent in some of her work. Fear, perhaps, or shyness. At other times she internalizes the world and writes of it indignantly. Her best work is courageous, but sometimes she uses only the courage of compulsion.

Many people at the concerts are old. Pensioners. They sit on benches beneath carefully pruned sycamores that stand in long rows to form a canopy of leaves. Some tourists come, attracted from the nearby Japanese tea garden. Many families attend. There are always girls looking for husbands and men looking for girls. They are shy on these days, perhaps because the band evokes a sense of earlier days which held the strictures of thou-shalt-not. They glance covertly at each other and seem trying to bolster their courage to express mutual longing. The wiser or more desperate girls have pet dogs on leashes. The dogs are good emissaries. Marriages are surely arranged by poodle, dachsund, and beagle.

There is a lonesomeness present. Not lonely. I always believe that the people will be lonely again on Monday morning when they return to their jobs through the big-city traffic. No. Lonesome, which I take to mean as not being at home and not being on loving ground. A great number of people in San Francisco were reared hundreds or thousands of miles away. The westward migration is larger than ever. I look at them and wonder why they came; their only tie to Cleveland or Wheeling, the telephone cables across the Rockies, the familiar handwriting on a letter. Then I think that they had no notion when they came of walking through a park on Sunday, walking through murmuring crowds where their singleness has a Goya starkness; the effect of unmasked sunlight flooding white concrete. They pre-empt the scenery.

Worse, the families are that way. They come together, men and women and children, with dogs and an occasional cat. They move privately and speak of private matters. There is no sense of community. Instead, there is fragmentation so that the crowd becomes units of one with feet that point outward and lips that speak away. I feel these things generally. In the specifics they are not always true. Sometimes there is a special occasion, Irish-American day, Hungarian day. Then there is a feeling of community that makes the starkness of the alone people a special painfulness to watch.

It was that way with the girl in the orange hat. She is a tall girl of slight figure who is eternally twenty-eight because she has not dared to become older.

When we first saw her we were sitting on the lawn. I was sketching. The girl came down steps leading in the direction of the art museum which houses the Brundage collection. The collection is a proud mix of good and bad. See it if possibile.

She came slowly, magnificently postured. At first I did not see. My wife directed my attention.

"Look," she said, "Sacagawea. I love her." My wife's inheritance is a mix of Mexican-Spanish-Indian. Enough to help her beauty. Enough also to make her conscious of the beauty in either distinct or modified racial traits. She looks for particularity of beauty.

"Sacagawea was probably short and fat," I told her. "She had white babies." I regretted my speech. My wife's enthusiasm was registering as I spoke. Perhaps the sunlight made my mind lazy. I tried to call it back.

"The lower lip . . . ."

"Is perfect," she told me. We have been married long enough for her to know what constitutes apology. A gift for understanding.

Men place trust as well as speak of it when they marry. I understand good fortune.

The girl was splendid. Her heritage probably lay in North Carolina or Oklahoma, if Cherokee. If not, then Creek or from one of the tall and beautiful peoples of the Northeast. I have seen it before, but seldom, the serenity implied by features. Rounded high cheeks, deep eyes, and an unusual small excessiveness about the mouth that is not sensuous but hints of thrill. A classical nose, a fine forehead, she would be a fit subject to be painted by genius. A second rate painter would tremble.

Her hair was black. Soft, long and black. It was the classical notion of Indian hair and she had been good enough to leave it that way. Her color was frail white. Translucent. Third generation. Fourth generation.

"By Indian parents, by parents the same," my wife murmured. "Look at her walk, it didn't come from the avenues."

And it did not. The posture did not come from schoolyard playgrounds where tall girls stoop to their self-consciousness. There was absolute fluidity in the walk. It was as smooth as the joyous movement of an otter.

The girl did not seem joyous. There was a passive reserve. It was not until she passed near and we saw her eyes that we pondered interior questions. Her eyes were dark and intense, eyes that I saw as filled with brooding and confusion. If she painted I would know. The deep things come out and rough up the conception. Even Renoir. The girl passed and was soon lost in the crowd, although for a time we could trace her by the flash of her orange knit dress and the small orange hat low against her dark hair.

"It is necessary to love," my wife said as we walked from the park to find our car. She seemed trying to remain detached but her voice was sad. "We all feel what that girl knows, or most do who have learned to sense as well as think. It's cruel to be alone."

"You always know too much." I smiled and dug for my keys, watching her because she was speaking and because she is beautiful. Her hair is also long. Her hair is dark; deep, and it fills my face when I love her. It fills my mind when I think of her.

"You don't have to meet someone to know them," she said.

She pleases me with story telling. It is her gift.

We drove across Geary, then California, and through the Presidio. There are easier ways to get to North Beach but none better.

"She is more than thirty," my wife said. "She was raised in a small town or near a small town where there was no one except family. It's possible she did not enter school at the proper age. Maybe that still makes her afraid."

"Why?"

"Maybe she had nothing to wear. Perhaps there was no school. There may have been discrimination."

"Of course." From the top of the Presidio the bay was like a blue exclamation above the trees and yellow stuccoed army houses. "Look," I pointed. An aircraft carrier nosed from behind distant buildings, this according to the perspective.

"I know all about her."

"I meant the carrier, they do not come here often."

"I am telling about the girl." Her voice was not pressing, not sharp, and the edge in it was an asking.

"Does it mean that much?" I was surprised.

"Yes. Without you, she is me. Except for a few years of age and some general supposing I've just described what you already know of me."

"And I did not notice." It was alarming. Loving someone, you forget that they have lived beyond you, lived in other places at other times.

"My father was short and half-Mexican and had religion and children."

"His daughter became a poet."

"I take credit for that," she said, "and remember that the truth of a poem is not always consciously in the poet. There are deeper layers of the mind, and some of those layers are hungry."

"The girl has touched you deeply." I spoke quietly. The traffic was very heavy. My attention was constantly diverted.

"What does she want to misunderstand, or not know about people like us?"

"Us?" We were nearly home.

She would say nothing more. I parked the Porsche, we drank cappuccino and went to our apartment. That evening I listened to Bach who is fundamental and good. My wife worked in her room. The next day I went to the gallery.

It was to be one of my most successful weeks. I placed true work that was not bought on speculation. I worked on my copy of a Wyeth. My love is art and Americans make art. Wyeth and Arthur Miller have not been exceeded. I love beauty, an appreciator. That night my wife was absent. She works one night a week in adult education programs.

Aloneness is good sometimes. From our apartment it is possible to see a great part of San Francisco and the bay. With the arguable exceptions of Athens and Madrid it is the most beautiful city in the world.

I stood at the large windows. The bay was purple and green in the last lustre of fading light. The island lay like a stone. From the Marin County side lights began to appear. The Golden Gate, subject of thousands of poor paintings, stood defying paint in the smooth sheen of purpling water. Lights appeared on the Richmond Bridge. Turning, but not moving to the windows on the other side, I could see reflections of light in the tops of a few tall buildings. Our apartment is over the city. It would be necessary to cross the room to gaze into the streets where traffic, sex, and the famous restaurants spelled the occupations and excitements of the night-time city.

Some of my wife's work lay on a low table. I picked it up. Unfinished. Very abrupt, as she sometimes writes in anger or fear.

> Vacuity sits in state surveying plunder,
> and our lives are spent in dreams of Mercedes,
> of tampered forests with selected trees,
> that complement our roads . . . .

A fragment. We have spoken of this before, there is a bitterness in her about unnatural things that I do not understand. The constructions of men may be either ignored or used. A fine piece of engineering may be an exquisite thing. Precision automobiles are not the same as dishwashers. I do not understand her resentment.

When she returned I was glad. We went out for a late dinner. On the following Sunday we returned to the park.

We arrived early. The park seemed newly washed. Large sprinklers were still watering, the liquid arcs throwing crystal shatterings in the sunlight. We walked through the arboretum, allowing time for the grass to dry and the crowds to gather. My wife was abstracted. I respect her moods. Once, and I did not call her attention, there was a flash of orange far away on a cross path. We were to see the girl a little later.

She arrived about halfway through the band program, and she arrived with company. A younger man. It made me wish we had gone elsewhere. My wife was stunned.

They came down the same steps, passing between the ornamental plantings that border the short slopes. The flowers were orange and yellow and red. They would have framed her perfectly, except for the man. Her hat was again orange, but a different hat. She wore a light orange suit and she was a gentleness, a contrast to the man.

He was about thirty, dressed in expensive and tasteless clothes, an efficient haircut, and his eyes were not kind. His face was tense. His laugh loud. Doubtless a hard and honest worker; one who knew jokes, and resenting it, told them with near defiance because he did not understand the resentment.

"No," my wife said. She turned to me. "Stop her."

"You can't stop people from talking and walking together."

"I'll stop her." She stood, walked to the couple and spoke to them. The man looked like a plastic pressing of a poor sculpture beside the woman. For one shocking moment I was unable to distinguish between the two women, unable to believe that I knew one less intimately than the other.

The couple was nearly amazed. I am a San Franciscan and know San Franciscans. We may even applaud the unorthodox but we do not intrude on one another. It was slightly embarassing, and then my wife returned with them. Three outlanders. Two were beautiful.

The girl's name was Marie. I thought of Catholic missions. The man's name was Jim and they had just met.

He appraised me and spoke of his job while watching my wife. I watched both women in turn.

"Have you just arrived in the city," I asked her. The band was playing a march. The man was humming.

"Nearly a year." She was very close. Her accent held touches of the red-neck South that did not match her low and musical voice. There is a vast range of southern accents.

"What do you want?" The man had stopped humming. He was using the 'no nonsense' voice of someone asking a price.

"To talk," my wife said. "Our custom on Sunday is to try to spend some time with another couple." There was a remarkable hatred in her voice. The Spanish intonations never quite leave. It was low, easily misunderstood, but the girl reacted. Watching. The man leaned forward. Interested. Too interested. I guessed his thought and was repulsed.

"Florida," I said, and turned to the girl.

"Kentucky, near the Tennessee line. I have to go now."

"Wait." My wife reached and nearly touched her. "I want to know you and that is a true thing."

"Chicago," the man said, "and before that Indianapolis."

The band crashed and cymbaled to a halt.

"How you must miss the mountains." I spoke carefully. "They are not as rugged as our western chain."

"Mountains?" The man was startled. "In Illinois?"

"No." The girl turned from my wife. Her face was tense, hard, and filled with restraint that would otherwise be tears. "They move like waves and they have trees all the way to the top," she said.

She walked rapidly away. The man followed, caught up with her, and together they passed into the crowd and from our view. The band began a blaring show tune. My wife stood quietly.

"They have only just met," I told her. "The girl is searching, not trapping. There is time for judgment."

"There has been time."

"I hope I understand." I folded the blanket and stood beside her.

"I love her for being beautiful. Unique. I love that."

"I love it too. She is like you."

She looked at me and there were tears and gentleness, her soft hair partly obscuring her face. There was something else. My mind was assailed with a sudden horror. There was also a terrifying, a pagan impression of submission.

We walked in silence across the park. Usually I hold her hand because it is warm and narrow and beautiful. On this day I did not hold her hand and it seemed inestimably precious. The girl in the orange hat would be making initial decisions now, decisions that perhaps could be recalled.

"Then I am failing." My voice was low.

"No. There is very much success. Please, let's smile."

She attempted a smile and I took her hand. We found the car and drove tonelessly through the sunlit streets between tall buildings that seemed monuments to easy and countless successes. The traffic was heavy and fast, continuous surprises of brightly painted steel. The sun reflected from tall columns of a thousand windows where men spoke of stocks and construction and insurance. I wondered, troubling, uncertain for the first time in our lives together. I tried to imagine just what were her inner and most unspeakable sorrows.

The Forest Ranger

The view from the freeway was excellent. Beyond the dusty trees, mottled and sickly from either fumes or disappointment, lay a narrow strip of San Francisco Bay on which cast-off bottles bobbed and shimmered softly in the diminishing light. The sunset would be sickening.

Near the water was an auto wrecking yard, a big one that processed junkers wholesale; stomping and kicking and mashing and baling them to be stacked on railway flatcars. It was instructional. No fewer than seventy klunks were fitted on each car, like multi-colored cans of anchovies. He had been counting them for half an hour.

Traffic moved. He pressed the accelerator and rolled forward twelve feet. He figured that the evening commuter jam was breaking. Only fifteen minutes ago he had moved five feet. He savored the recollection. It had given him a good look at the baler.

With the daily salvation in sight he sat thoughtfully; distinguished, holding down the seat of the Brooks Brothers. He sat in the expensive automobile. He sat listening attentively to the imported radio that was not playing. It was buzzing. He had tuned out the helpful helicopter announcer who advised him to avoid the only road that led home. The idea almost made sense. He tuned back to the station. The announcer was still speaking of congestion. This time it was of the eliminatory tract. He reflected that it was a long way between filling stations and wriggled uncomfortably in his seat. Then he tuned the announcer out and chuckled. A man well under forty should learn exquisite control of all things . . . the girl in the car next to him smiled. He decided that she should go topless.

The parking lot lunged forward. It was dazzling. He was nearly past the baler now and thinking of Yellowstone. The park. Ten years ago, a kid, he had wanted to be a forest ranger. His old man had encouraged him. His old man had been in the insurance game and must have known. Who ever heard of an uptight bear? A squirrel in the wrong bag? What in the hell had happened to them? Him? His old man? In spite of his bladder he chuckled again.

He chuckled with the secret glee of a man content to know an impending revenge, a man to whom the rage of an outraged wife was a trifle. She suspected him of an affair. He allowed her to believe that. It was much cleaner than working with the truth. Besides, he was afraid of making counter-accusations. Maybe only birds and elephants mated for life.

Revenge. He rolled the flavor of the antique word across his tongue. It tasted good. He was now a man. He wondered why automobiles were not fitted with chamber pots. Then he marveled again at the magnificent luck that had served to bring him the means of stunning violence; the means to be the prime adulterer of a way of life that understood adultery to be as healthful as breakfast cereal. His name was Arthur. It had been for three months. Before that it had been Art. He thought on the old days. They were disgusting. Art and Arthur were both fed up.

Three months. Three little months since the huge moving van had pulled up to his door to gulp his possessions; piano, fishing rods, bed (dismantled, dismasted, depleted), rugs, pictures, college artifacts, tables, television, books, record player, potted plants, objects dart, all . . . gobbled into the maw of the fathomless, infathomable giant.

He had spoken to the driver. Wiry man. Tough. No fat.

"You'll take good care . . . ."

"Of everything," the driver told him. "Except the potted plants. We don't never guarantee the potted plants."

"The wife . . . ."

"She rides with you."

"Yes," he had admitted, and turned to the truck which fascinated him. "Big."

"Fifty feet long. Over three thousand cubic feet capacity. Up to forty-two thousand gross." The driver had been proud of his machine. They walked through the empty rooms, checking to see that nothing had been left.

"You see a lot of road?"

"Eighty, maybe a hundred thou a year. You going into the business?"

The thought startled him. "No, going to California. Bucked for one grade and got promoted two. Nice surprise. Going to California. Twenty thousand a year."

"Yeah," the driver shook his head in commiseration. "Won't make more myself. But," he brightened, "it's been an off year."

"Can you make that much?" He had been incredulous.

"Sure. But lots of road. Never home. Fella like you it's different. Good money and home every night."

"Uh huh," he said, trying to feel a good-bye. The trees beyond the window were bare. Sterile. The house was empty. There were no whispers. "Listen," he asked, "is it nice there like they say? A little peace . . . ."

"They grow artichokes," the driver told him.

The truck had continued to fascinate him. He and his wife drove the new automobile coast to coast. During most of the first day he stayed with the truck. His wife wanted to check up on the trucker's driving. It was a relief. On the second day he was sleepy and pulled over early.

His wife protested. "If a little guy like him can go, why can't . . . ."

"They take dope," he had offered hopefully, knowing that it was going to be a pretty long trip.

The traffic moved. Two whole car lengths. He checked his watch and congratulated himself on his progress. He was either ten minutes or fifteen hundred feet ahead of schedule.

The trip had started long. At about Minnesota it had shortened. His wife had loved him again by Minnesota. They had taken time to explore the country and ended by exploring each other. Like back in college and then later when they were married.

"Please," she had said. "I love you," she had said. He thought a lot about Minnesota.

In California the biggest change was the weather. That, and artichokes were plentiful. His job was more responsible. He had to push hard from the first. It filled his life. Later there was time for a drink before lunch. The clubs were a little more liberal. The women, maybe. He still went home every night. Now he drove. No more commuted trains. The prestigious new car was a joy on weekends when there was a chance to drive in the hills. Sometimes his wife accompanied him. She was very busy. Clubs, entertainment, art lessons, politics. She no longer said please.

He tried Reno, then Tahoe. His wife loved both, the excitement, the crowds, the color, the gambling. He decided that she was a bum. In New York it had been bridge. In the west it was nickel slots. A take down. A come down. A bust.

And prices were high. Lord, Lord how high were prices. He started bucking for the next grade and thought of a mistress. In shopping he found that even the idea was expensive.

Far past the baler now. Soon there would be a gentle curve. Sunset would find him overlooking the sanitary landfill. Traffic settled into a reluctant five-mile crawl; hesitating, sometimes speeding up, making conforming ripples of start, stop, brake-light and screech.

It was really the traffic that got him. Finally, he had to admit that it was really the traffic. People were about the same. His wife had returned to New York Normal. But he was not the same. Something of him responded to the mountains, looked toward the sea, remembered Minnesota.

And the traffic never ceased. Once, returning home from an ordinary party at 3 A.M. on a Tuesday he had waited five minutes before daring to cross a street. Traffic. Traffic.

He remembered the truck wistfully. The driver. A hundred thousand miles a year. A hundred thousand. One night with pencil and paper he figured that he would drive to work and home not less than fifteen hours a week, fifty weeks a year. Seven hundred fifty hours. More than thirty days. Twice his vacation. In that time he would cover, well, he would cover almost five thousand miles. There was no question of moving from the high-speed, commute community and expensive house. The office would peg him a loser. He thought about the truck. One day, glancing through the classified, he had seen an ad which explained how he, too, could be a Big Rig Man. The idea was loathsome.

What he needed was a cabin in the forest. Deer playing. A stream. Trees. Maybe a farm. Sunlight. A loving woman. The bit.

His wife was blonde. He thought a lot about brunettes. Thought on thought. Passion unexpended. He clipped the ad and shuddered. It was several days before he understood his motives.

He planned a final gesture. Perverse. The highest violence he could conceive. Then he and his blonde wife could leave forever. There were other ways to live, other places; Australia, Iowa, Manitoba. Maybe she would go with him. There was some money saved. Some. They could cash in the insurance. Maybe she would not go with him. It was the traffic that was the cause, or maybe it was the traffic that was fruition. There is no race when the rat won't run.

On the following Saturday he had gone to the driving school.

Monster trucks stood around. The biggest one . . . . "That one," he said to the friendly proprietor who eyed his check with the same cold eye he turned on the nineteen dollar lite-weight casuals. "Call me Art," he explained timidly to the honest proprietor.

"Not that one," the man explained. He pointed to a different truck. "That one's for beginners. You start there if you aim to bust gears."

The truck had been old and small, but homey. It smelled of stale tobacco, sweat, and things discarded from lunches carried in paper bags. In a single lesson he had learned all ten gears and how to shift them. His shift was lumpy. On the following week he returned. His shift improved. In three weeks he could drive but not maneuver. He needed to know how to maneuver.

"You're really serious, fella." The man was even more friendly: the checks were clearing. "What the hell," he grinned. "Take out the big one."

A concession. An advancement. The big one turned out to be easier than the smaller one. When he backed it made a longer lever, easier to judge. There was a great feeling of fascination and satisfaction. His bank statement showed checks to M. Jones for services. His wife began talking of people named Marie and Muriel. He could not explain and was afraid to challenge. She seemed very busy, desperately busy, yet there were some things for which anyone could make time . . . not that he cared. That was the trick. Care only for the drama and a decent exit.

Twice he left work on some pretext, learning how to drive, how to jack the huge van down simulated alleys, against simulated curbs, through simulated mountain passes which were perfectly flat but horribly curved. He was an apt student. He was awarded a degree.

They offered to find him a job. He refused. He did not want to drive a truck. He only wanted to *know how* to drive a truck. The plan. Maybe his wife would not go with him.

He speeded up because traffic speeded up. Now his car was going thirty. Soon he was up to forty. Then he came to the correct ramp and turned for home, the auto lights searching through the early darkness. The new car was a good car but lately it seemed puny. His big rig degree (hidden between leaves of *Games People Play*) was warranty against the smallness of life. It was insurance. It was power.

When he arrived home there was a note. He was to meet his

wife for dinner and a party. He had forgotten about that party. To dress was a matter of minutes. To shave was a matter of deliberation, then planned forgetfulness. Hipster, hip . . . he would grow a beard and wear lumberjack shirts. He was tired. He wanted to sit in the sun, wanted to get quietly loaded, wanted, wanted. Instead he allowed himself a quick one before returning to the car and broaching the evening.

Coming from the drive he waited for a car to pass. Then he waited for another car to pass. Then he entered traffic and decided that tomorrow was the day. Tomorrow was Friday. Fridays were excellent days for endings. At the party he would drink with care. A sure hand.

At the party his wife was cool. Maybe the forgotten shave. Maybe the bank statements. His wife danced three times with a chubby man named Vernon. Trucker Art drank. He watched the shapeliness of his wife and refused to worry. There was no affair after all. If she was looking, she had found no one yet.

No affair. Vernon used the same freeway, worked the same hours. No time. Trucker Art fuzzily mulled a vague sorrow for Vernon who was never going to make out, either. Then he felt an absolute sorrow for himself. It felt like New York. It did not feel like Minnesota. He was a little over his limit when they went home and slept.

"Today," he said when he woke up.

"Don't wake me," she told him. "Why today?"

"It's past time."

"I agree. You woke me up. Time for what?" She put her hand against his face.

He checked his watch on the nightstand. He was a little behind schedule. Everything must look normal. Nothing must go wrong. Nothing. "Go back to sleep," he told her.

She went back to sleep. No breakfast. He swilled coffee and orange juice. Smoked cigarettes. He got in his car and drove for an hour and a half; checked into the office; checked out of the office. "Later," he told the receptionist, with neat ankles who looked as if she hoped for a double meaning.

"Liar," he told himself and looked at his desk before he left. Wife's picture, she smiling. Pretty when she smiled. Embossed desk set. Monogrammed pen given by former secretary on his promotion. Lucky piece. Clutter. Crap. He slipped the picture into a pocket and went down to his car. "Sentimentalist," he told himself. "Fool. She will throw you out."

He paused to light a cigarette. He squinted over the tilted butt, looking at the executive parking lot through smoke. "I am a desperate man," he told himself, "the next Vernon will be someone without a commute."

He paused again. Surprised. "So that's the reason, after all. Not revenge. The grand gesture and leave? No. The big wake-up and win, or throw and crap-out."

He climbed in the car reading the sign that shimmered from his imagination across the windshield. *One Owner Repo—Take Over Payments.* It was a beautiful car. He thought that he would miss the car. He started the engine and drove aimlessly, across cable car tracks, through the beautiful park, into the chatter of Chinatown and the erotica and pizza of North Beach. The beautiful city. Well, he would miss those parts. But on the other face he had been missing them anyway. At two-thirty he changed to working clothes in a service station. At three o'clock he was at the rental agency to keep his appointment.

It was a huge truck. The instrument of question, after all, and not of revenge. It was a premium instrument. Fully as long as the mover's. Fifty feet. Fifty feet. It stood grumbling on the ready-line, huge, snouty. He did not want a tilt cab. Long. A conventional. Long.

The gears came in smoothly and made him proud. He moved into traffic, standing high above traffic. Look down. Cars going by. Girls' knees, fat men's paunches, kids waving from rear windows, yappy dogs. And smooth, those gears. He made the freeway easily and thought that it was not bad at three o'clock. The traffic was heavy like always, but moving. He wheeled the rig like an expert.

The traffic was moving too well. It threw him ahead of schedule. He slowed down and a cop tailed him. A speed up and the cop passed. He slowed down again. Cars crackled around him blatting horns. He was afraid one would run under the trailer.

With the speed back up the schedule was shot. He entered the approach to the main bridge that carried traffic for half of the city. The bridge that handled eighty thousand cars a day. The bridge that was a whole five lanes wide. It was a beautiful bridge. A man could buy a postcard . . . .

He paid his toll and continued across the bridge to drive into the hills. The engine roared big against the grades. He down-shifted the gears. The hills spilled wild flowers. The speed caused a tiny vibration in his driving mirror that glinted sunshine. He played with the giant and enjoyed the exhaust crack, coasting hills, tapping the brakes to hear them hiss, testing the air horns. He liked it more than any car. Very comfortable. Easier to handle at speed. He confidently turned it around and played all the way back to the bridge where he entered the ramp headed back into the city.

He decided to do it immediately. He slowed.

Traffic boomed around him. He was blocking the curb lane at five miles per hour. He slowed to a stop. Traffic backed up behind him. He cut the wheel hard left and eased the cab across the next lane. Traffic backed up more. Loud honking. He checked and then eased the truck into an oncoming lane. The trailer was huge in his mirrors, swinging across two lanes while the cab blocked the third. Traffic screeching and trying to by-pass. Ease across the fourth lane. Violent yelling. Screeching of brakes. No bumps.

He pulled straight across the bridge to block all five lanes. Pandemonium.

The cops would come. The getaway was important. He had to hurry. He climbed down and locked the cab. Maybe someone would leave a car and attack him. No one did. "Sheep," he told the rapidly lengthening line of cars, "Lemmings." He raised the hood to the accompaniment of crying horns and took the distributor cap. He threw it and the key into the bay. The two miles of bridge were nearly full. Cars turning around, trying to go back. Dinged fenders. Hollering. He looked at the truck. It was a beautiful truck. It was a beautiful bridge. They looked good together.

He checked his watch. Four-thirty. Going home time.

He stepped to the pedestrian walk to stroll from the bridge. A breeze caught his hair and he smiled in the din of horns. Far out on the bay a white glint of afternoon sun came from a billowing sail. The sea. The hills.

He wondered what his wife would do. As he walked beside the magnificent view, in triumphant parade before the salutation of horns, he found himself framing arguments that would persuade her to leave with him.

I Take Care of Things

It was late beyond the usual time of the sirens. I sat on the driver's side of the cruiser waiting for Frank to quit heaving. Our light was flashing a circular beacon into the blackness of the surrounding trees. We were just inside the park. The light made a changing red glow in the trees and pulled darkness behind it like a vacuum. The trees were moving in a light wind and spitting a few leaves. The light ticked, rotating. My hands were tense. There had been a wreck. Two kids on a motorcycle had missed a curve at speed. One was a girl. She had been thrown against a guy wire. They must have rapped into the curve at sixty-plus. It had been a big bike.

Fire equipment was parked fifty yards down the road. A fireman in a yellow slicker leaned hard on the straight stream nozzle that could whip the hose like snapping steel cable if it got loose. The water hit the pavement and bounced into a spray of red from the emergency lights.

Between us and the fire truck another fireman came from behind some trees. His face seemed paler in the flash of red than in the darkness. He steadied himself against a tree. Then he stepped onto the road. I eased back in the seat and watched. Pretty soon we could go.

Frank was getting quiet. He sat with the car door open and his feet in the road. He raised his head like he was testing himself. Then he wiped his mouth with his shirt sleeve. He touched his hand to his shirt front and dropped his hand fast. He had pulled the boy out from the broken frame of the motorcycle.

"I will," I told him. I reached to unbutton the shirt which had a lot of blood on front. The blood was cold and slick. It is always a strange feeling. I opened the buttons down to his belt. He pulled the tail out of his pants and got the rest. He jerked the shirt off and balled it up, throwing it on the floor in back.

"Your badge," I told him.

"Screw the badge," he said, "and you, too." His voice was close to hysteria. He got out of the wet undershirt by pulling up and holding it away from his face. His hair was pushed around. He was getting bald toward the front. The thin side hair tangled and stood up. His brows were heavy and looked messed. Probably they looked like that because his eyes were wild. He was only thirty-three or four, but he looked like a crazy man of sixty.

"I'll get the badge," I told him.

"And the rest of the world."

"Everybody, huh."

"Them, too. Leave me alone."

He is older than I am by a couple of years. In some ways he is younger because he never learns. At least his feelings never learn. I saw him break up once before. Cops are wrong to break up.

"Be back," I told him and climbed from the car. The ambulance was being loaded. They were about finished. I walked to the back of the ambulance. The guys were not careful.

The driver was an old man, very tall if he would straighten up, but he was stooped. His gray hair was streaked red and black in the lights. His helper was a kid. The kid looked wrong. Almost like a head. He looked high.

"You ready?" Their job was bad. You could tell about the body. Across the bridge of her nose there was a scrape that was nearly bloodless.

The driver looked at me. He was about to close the door. "Nearly ready. You want to check it?"

"No need."

"No need to hurry either," the kid said, and grinned. He was tall like the driver. His hair was too long. It was black and was slicked against his head. His hands were manicured. A homosexual maybe, or something different. All kinds of perversion hang around death. Up close you could tell he was high. He giggled.

"You like it." I watched him. He stopped giggling. His eyes looked all right except that they were excited. He was not high on drugs.

"No," he said. His voice was trying to go low and serious. He could not quite get it down there.

"Sure he does," the driver said. He was old and looked old. Ambulance guys working a big city are usually losers. Paid by the shift. Sleep in.

"Come over here," I told him. We walked away from the ambulance and toward the cruiser. About midway I stopped. There was no reason to let him see Frank.

"Make an inventory?"

"Didn't you?" He looked indignant. I gave him a leaf of paper from my book because the forms were in the car. He began scribbling, using the back of the book. They had custody of a couple of watches, a billfold, and a few bucks currency. "He doesn't steal," the old man said, "and I don't need to." He was hot. It was my job.

"He ride in back?" I pointed to the kid.

"Sometimes. He don't always ride with me."

"With live ones?"

"I ride with the live ones. He don't go with me all the time. I don't know what he does with other guys." He knew trouble, that old man. He signed the paper and gave it to me. There was a kicked look in his eyes. He wanted to say something and either did not know how or did not know what.

"Sorry about the list," I told him. He turned and walked back to the ambulance. The helper climbed in the riding side and they pulled away. Before they were around the curve the old man secured his light.

It was about wrapped up. The firemen had pressure off the hose. I was going to ask them to shoot under our car but it was too late. Instead, I walked to where the girl had hit. A human has a lot of blood. The pavement was clean under the lights. Beside the road the gravel was gone. It had been washed back into the grass. The roadside was slick with mud. Grass was beaten down and washed out in one big area. There is a lot of pressure on those hoses. Later on the park crews would come around and sod. Maybe they would not even know why the grass was washed out. Maybe they would bitch. It was clean. A good job.

I waved to the nearest fireman and went back to the car. When I climbed in Frank looked better. He was still not good but he seemed to have some control. He was sitting straight, not slumped over. His arms were muscular but his chest was kind of puny and thin. His chest was heaving. It looked like a contradiction after seeing his arms.

"I'm sorry," he said. He looked straight ahead.

"Sorry is for kids," I told him. "I'll take you home. They don't need for you to check in naked."

"Taking a chance."

"Can't you tell the difference? Taking no chance. The shift's out in an hour anyway." I drove to the edge of our sector before calling in to report the scene clear. Then I took us out of service. It was past four-thirty Thursday morning. A loose time. Even if I was seen I could explain.

"Coffee," I told Frank. I pulled beyond an all-night restaurant and walked back. The counterman was sitting and reading a magazine. I have known him for a couple of years. He can guess things, the way guys can sometimes when they are used to being alone. He looked up when I walked in.

"Hi, Burns," he said. "You had a bad one." He stood up and poured coffee in two paper cups. He did it slow. Rheumatism.

"Bad enough." I leaned on the counter. The walk-boards in back of the counter looked greasy and slick.

"I heard the noise." He is not a nosy guy. He was just asking if I needed anything besides coffee.

"Make it black," I told him. "You ought to wipe this counter." I had leaned in a spot of mustard or some kind of slop. The counter was cracked linoleum, dark green where it was not peeling.

He passed me the coffee. "What a crappy job," he said. By the time I was through the doorway he was reading the magazine again.

Frank spilled some of the coffee in his lap. It scalded and he sat still. Probably it helped steady him. Then he started drinking the coffee and that helped more. A pretty fair cop, Frank. But, wrong-headed. He relates. Takes it personal. When he first saw that body I know he thought of his daughter. She is thirteen and healthy and does not ride on motorcycles. He thinks muddled. He gets one thing on his mind and it means something else. At first I thought it was morals. He would lose his temper. I've seen him beat a pusher into the hospital and the guy was only dealing in pot. It is not morals. He relates.

"I got something to tell you," he said. His voice still sounded lousy. There was a tremble like someone who was crying.

"I probably don't want to hear." I drank off the rest of my coffee and pulled away. It was true. I did not want to hear because he gave me an uneasy feeling. Something he had done had made no sense. Fooling around.

When we got to the scene we had checked the kids out fast. I went to run traffic by and chase the ghouls off. When they did not leave I put our spotlight on the girl and that got rid of some of them. Frank had been in the bushes freeing the boy's body. The ambulance guys could have done that.

"I got to tell you," he said.

"Save it."

"Now." The more he talked the worse his voice got.

We rode for a while. It was less dark. Not light really. It was the way it looks just before you get the first far-off suggestion of dawn. Frank leaned forward like he was completely exhausted.

"Listen," he said, "put yourself in my place."

"There ain't no amount of money."

His voice got on a low monotone. Probably he figured to control it that way.

"I looked at the boy," he said, "and you went out to the road. Then I went and looked at the girl. Clean cut. Surgical."

"Forget it."

"I got mad. Cars backed up. People walking off to puke and then coming back for another look. Just a little girl."

"Everything dead looks little." I looked at him because I was hearing something. His hands were out of control. His eyes were wild again. His mouth hung open. He was panting like a dog. That was what I was hearing. A dog pant. His control was gone and suddenly, right there, I hated him. It was a strange feeling.

"Get it over," I told him. I could not remember hating anyone like that before.

"Went back to the boy. Big hump of stuff in the bushes. Part human and part iron. Wedged into the bushes getting madder. That girl. Hating. Crying. Started to swear. Felt for a pulse."

"Found one, didn't you?"

He turned to me, shocked out of his panting. I had him cut from under. "Yes, light pulse."

"Thanks." I looked out at the street. We were near his house. "So you got mad and turned the whole mess upside down like you were pulling out a body. That what you wanted to tell me?" I was ahead of him. It wrecked his climax.

"His back was broken. It twisted and then there wasn't any more pulse." He was gasping so hard he could hardly breathe. He could not say anything more. I drove. It was only a couple of blocks.

Death. You work with it. Sometimes it's dirty like when a drunk goes out in an alley. Sometimes it's painful. Old people with heart attacks. Automobile injuries that bleed them white and cold before you can get it stopped. Gas. Fire. Drowning.

I pulled up to his house. He did not move.

"You want me to decide," I told him. "You want me to make it right by doing something. Make up your mind for you." I hated him.

"You know what it is."

"Well, the hell with you. Get the coroner's report."

"You know the word. You know what it is."

"Sure, the word is that it's five-thirty in the morning and I need sleep." I turned to him. "Okay, give me your gun."

He passed it over like he was glad. He was actually breathing better. I dropped the gun between the seat and the door on my side. "Get out," I told him. He got out like he did not understand. I reached over and slammed the door.

"Get some sleep," I told him. I shoved it in gear and got away before he could answer. The gun was beside the seat. He could not shoot himself. Instead, he was going to have to stand in the growing light without a shirt. The whole world chases itself in an eighty-mile-an-hour frenzy. He could match his mind to that along with whatever he called a conscience. He could walk to the nearest precinct or he could damned well go in the house to his wife, take a shower, and go to bed.

There was the beginning traffic. Milkmen and other route guys. I felt better than I had for an hour. Leaving Frank like that was a help. It had been uncomfortable when I hated him.

Land

"My grandpa, my drinking grandpa, not the preacher, came to these parts just after the Civil War. The land was taken. He married a widow to get land. She had almost two sections. It's a good thing, I guess. He would have killed to get land.

"I like to think of him. Scandalous old rip. He started a little general store down by the crossroads. There's a town there now. Made a living off the store and a fortune off the land.

"Caused scandal too. Use to have a little two-horse rig, surrey painted red and white like a circus and ran a matched tandem that never saw a plow. Ran it into town, the horses stepping high and easy, pocking along the road out there which would have been dust in those days. The horses were white, of course, and the leather was deep worked and beautiful, decorated in red. You can see yourself how it would have been, them horses, head high and pulling that dinky little rig.

"Take it into town, the horses snorting and that rig gleaming like he'd captured the sun. Pull it up in front of the courthouse like an English squire. People flock around. Him blowing and taking on, making like it wasn't nothing. Then, by and by, he'd disappear and you could bet some family had trouble. Awful good man with the girls, my grandpa was. Awful bold. Painted his fence posts white and gave them red caps of barn paint. Caused about as much scandal as his women.

"But my dad was different. Loved the land just as much, kind of hated the store and so after while it went down hill. He never took much after grandpa. Steady man. Use to hitch up a team once a month and drive it into town. He'd bring back the news and supplies to sell in the store. I still remember cracker barrels, tub cheese; still remember.

"And I like to think of my dad, like I like to think of grandpa. But I picture him different, of course. Like to think of that old, old man as a young man, getting up on a clear morning, the taste of morning on his tongue and going out to the barn. Chilly morning maybe, frost hanging out across the fields like fallen fog. Him harnessing his work team to a spring wagon and heading into town.

"Sun coming up, burning off the frost, and my dad would sit behind that team, maybe not even driving because he owned good horses. Sitting there watching birds rise off a field where somebody had put in wheat. A quiet time. You know, he never questioned. Married, maybe happy, but never had to ask. There was only one thing he could be.

"Well, I ramble. You want to farm. Get your land and you'll still need twenty thousand dollars. Don't believe a man can do with less just starting from scratch. But, it needs more than that. More than that. There's the feel of things.

"I kind of see the land sometimes. Like in my head. And I've been on this land sixty-seven years. See it. Especially times like now. Crops worked, land lying healthy but resting, and you know it's healthy because you've worked and schemed it all out, what you'll do.

". . . like a crop I had in the early forties. Corn so high in the rich places that you walked through it like a forest. Twelve, fourteen feet tall. No corn like that now. Better yield but not so tall.

"No, you wait. I'll get there. You come here with money and a hunger in your eyes. I've seen it. Seen it, and men do get impatient. I'm tryin' to tell you.

"You go look at your fields. I know mine. Some land works

easier than others. You get a kind of gentle, easy strip down a field, or maybe a whole field that's like it wants to be turned. Field right beside can be a bastard. Work it up, fertilize, refertilize . . . nothing you do will make that field match the one across the road. Nothing but a road between. Before the road it was all the same.

"Yes, I know them. Wander through them like my dad used to when he worked the land. Sometimes it's like he lingered, you know. Old. Old when he died.

"And my grandpa. He built the barn with my dad helping after the first one burned. Lost most of their feed that year. Animals slaughtered against waste because grandpa wasn't going to neighbors for feed. Stiff-necked. Proud. I don't remember him too well.

"Well, you want to buy and I'm old now. Yes, I admit. You drove all this way to talk. Give an old man a minute more.

"I see him, you know. Sometimes on the land it's like I see him, bending down maybe to clear something from a fence row, or walking past the grove. Remember him young, like when he was teaching me. Full of interest. Full of plans. Coming in tired of a night. Not like later when he was sick . . . he got sick. Kind of took the starch out. Lingered awhile and then he died.

"I'm kind of sorry you came. I thought . . . well, don't keep many animals now. When the boys were here. But, there's no sense in that. Two good boys and both of them gone. One in Bridgeport, the other in Sarasota. Educated boys, but good ones too.

"I don't know. I'm sorry you came. I thought I could sell. Thought it all out and said, 'Yes, you must,' but I guess I can't. I'll give you the name of a fella I know. Hard up. Place run down a little. Maybe he'll deal. Mister, I'm sorry, I just can't sell this land."

Text and Notes on a Sermon
Preached in Harlan, Ky., Bluefield, West Va.,
Hamilton, Ohio, and elsewhere

"My text for the day is taken from Jeremiah, twenty-third chapter, sixteenth verse, in which the Lord is warnin his people to beware of false prophets. It is a good one for us to think about these days when so many of our young people are being persuaded from natural, God-like ways down the paths of temptation."

"Thus saith the Lord of hosts, Hearken not unto the words of the prophets that prophesy unto you; they make you vain: they speak a vision of their own heart, and not out of the mouth of the Lord."

"Walking over here on this beautiful Sabbath morning I could not help thinkin of a young man who came to me several years ago deeply troubled in spirit. This young man's parents had worked hard all their lives, were diligent and God-fearing and members of my parish in another town. Through all these years they worked, and when they were blessed with a son they praised God and began a little savings to see that the boy went through college. Because, dear friends, they had never received the blessings of a good education and were determined that their boy was not goin to be hindered in his life's work like they had been.

"Well, the boy grew and he was a good boy. He attended the Sunday School and Church regular. Many's the time I'd look over the congregation; striving to reach out to them, and see this boy's blond hair shining in a shaft of sunlight coming through the stained glass windows. A serious boy and a good one. I would see him like he was already in God's Holy light, see him in my imagination like it made a halo around and about him; and I would think to myself, 'Surely this is one of the Lord's annointed.' And I tell you it made me try harder, made me work for the salvation of that congregation.

"Because all around that boy were other people who were also sittin in God's sunlight, but it did not transform them. They were Pharisees, men who came each Sunday to service, men who gave much money to the church, but men who gave none of their time, none of the commitment of their lives or immortal souls for the praise of God's majesty. Sometimes I would look at that boy and think, 'Him, he is the only one who hears, and if my maker calls me now and says, "Reverend, show me that flock which you have gathered unto me," I would have to point shamefully at that boy and admit in God's presence that there was only one, one single, solitary, immortal soul of which I was sure.' And I would have to bow my head with guilt, as we are all guilty in the face of the living God, and beg forgiveness that the talent entrusted to me had reaped such little gain. One soul. And I was younger then.

"The boy grew and I remember the day he left for college, his old mother crying but happy and his father proud. They had asked me and I told them about a small school in a distant town that I knew was run by fair and God-fearing men. The boy went and the following spring he returned . . . ."

Continuation of the Text circa 1937

". . . the following spring he returned.

"You all remember those days, remember the twenties when the American people fled from their churches in the countryside to the Sodoms of the cities. Some of you were seduced by the temptation. There was much money, and though nothing is wrong with money, there was much love of money and what it would buy. And it is right there that the people of America sinned in the eyes of Almighty God. It is there that the cornerstone was laid for the present trouble. For God looked down and saw the evil, the drinking, the whoring, the dirt that his people were leaving on the land; the rutting and disease and the destruction of souls, and he saw that the evil was Money. And God said, 'I will take the money and punish the people and make them poor so that they may rid themselves with their guilt and poverty. Thus are the sins of the fathers visited upon the sons, yea, even unto the third and fourth generations.' And God sent a great depression and the people crawled beneath the wrath of God and returned themselves to their homes.

"The boy also returned. During that summer, all summer, he came each Sunday to church. But he did not come to see his Pastor. I watched, trembling in my heart, because as the boy sat there, his hair still golden in the colored sunlight, he somehow seemed changed. And I prayed to God in his infinite mercy, prayed that the boy would have strength and that he would come to see me; that he would come and that I would have the wisdom to relieve the great burden that God had chosen to lay on his heart.

"My prayers were answered. Before he left for his second year of school he visited me and his mind was filled with trouble.

"There was an Evil at his college. The Devil chooses many kinds of men for his purpose and this time the Devil had chosen a clever man, an educated man filled with superstition and the Asp of questioning. This man was a teacher at the college and by his teaching betrayed his evil. When the boy returned the man was gone, dismissed to wander through his own branches of faithlessness and Hell where he will howl for all eternity. His guilt could not be forgiven. He destroyed faith.

"This man was the disciple of another who had fallen. I know that many of you will have heard the name, the name of a minister of God who was tempted by wealth and honor and reputation to sell his soul. That man's name was Emerson and the teacher believed his writings.

"There are many false prophets and some of them are alive today. Some of them are still having their writings read and talked about. One of them—God grant you never find—is Robert Inger-soll who scoffed at God and is now dead under God's almighty hand.

"The reading of philosophy is hard. It is easy to misunderstand. I will tell you about what this Emerson wrote and you can decide. He wrote and spoke sayin that God is not in the churches. Nature is God. You go into the forests and along the shore and there God speaks to you. And that is all, except . . . , listen careful to the blasphemy which I'm near afraid to pronounce, Except that Man is God.

"In other words he said that man is God and nature is God which means that both are the same thing, and you go out into nature—which is like going out into yourself, I reckon—and God speaks to you . . . but, since you are God and nature is God it looks to me like what Emerson meant was to go out in a field and talk to yourself. How much sense does that make?

"Many here are farmers. They know God. They see him in the tender green unfolding of the leaves of their crops. They know that His fingers touch the seed, give the sun, bring forth life from the earth. But, they know that for men the Holy congregation of the Spirit, the lifting of the voice in reverent prayer for forgiveness, prayer for the Glory of God, who, though man is a miserable worm beside Him, reaches His hand down to man as he reaches to the seed and says, 'Grow. Multiply. Give forth thy fruit in thy season.'

"The story has a beautiful ending. The boy came that day and the Lord granted me the wisdom to seek this passage, this warnin against false prophets. The boy returned to college sustained, studied hard and worked long hours to fulfill his promise in the Lord. He is now a minister of our church with a small parish in Memphis, Tennessee.

Continuation of the Text circa 1947

". . . the following spring he returned.

"You remember those days, remember the war when God raised His almighty hand gainst the pride of man. 'I will take the evil of money,' He said. And He took the wealth of the land and changed it to dross. And still the people stood stiff-necked and proud. They refused to bow to the will of the Lord. And Almighty God looked down and he was sorrowed and displeased and he said, 'I will send a deadly war and it will remove from every home some person. From some it will take the first born and kill him in battle. From others it will take the father, to die in the factories under the bursting bloom of molten steel. And from some it will take the home itself, that the families wander from city to city over the face of the earth; meeting only strangers; remembering and lamenting their neighbors, their lost loved ones, and their little patch of ground.

"And I will create a great machine of destruction so that the people will fear and will return to God and praise my name. For I have said that the sins of the fathers will be visited upon the sons, yea, even unto the third and fourth generation.

"So the boy returned, and during that short furlough of two weeks he came both Sundays to church. But he also came at night, troubled in his heart, standin outside the church and hidden in shadow where he thought no one could see. I watched, trembling, because the boy was under temptation and seemed changed. And I prayed to God that the boy would have strength, prayed that God would send him to me and that I might have the wisdom to relieve the great burden that God had chosen to lay on the boy's heart.

"My prayers were answered. Before he returned to the Army and to battle he visited me and his mind was filled with trouble.

"There were many Evils in the Army, drinking and gambling and whoring and sacrilege. There were many temptations and pagan ideas. There were Catholics and Jews and Atheists.

"The Devil chooses many kinds of men for his purpose and this time the Devil had chosen a man and given him power. The man was a non-commissioned officer in the boy's rifle squad. He taught and spoke as a disciple of a corrupt and evil man. When the boy returned he was strengthened and able to withstand the arguments of the officer who was later destroyed in battle and rests in Hell for all eternity.

"The man was a disciple of a false prophet of a false god; one that he called Logic. That man's name was Marx.

"There are many such false prophets in these days. They masquerade as government experts and scientists and call themselves complicated names like psychologist to help fool the people.

"The reading of philosophy is hard. It is easy to misunderstand. I will tell you what this Marx wrote and you may decide.

"Marx said that there is no God and that only man can create a heaven, and the place the heaven is to be created is right here on earth. Marx said that to have heaven it is necessary to grow more crops, build more houses, make more machines and clothes and tools. Then be sure that everybody gets the same share; that because people weren't going to like working while somebody else loafed, it was going to be necessary to kill some people and destroy their governments . . . and there had to be a lot of power to control the people until after heaven was built.

"Do you see how clever this is? He says to do some things that are good but he uses evil. The will of God is that 'The Poor shall be always with you' and the will of God promises everlasting life; yet Marx did not promise everlasting life, he denied God, and he was goin to make a heaven by building factories. How much sense does that make?

"Many of you here are farmers and shopkeepers. You know how hard it is to be responsible, how much it costs for equipment, and how your joyful tithe to the Lord is always worked hard for and seems little. You know the satisfaction of working all day, earning your bread by the sweat of your brow, and goin home at night to rest. You know the joy of coming to church on Sunday in Holy congregation of the Spirit, the lifting of the voice in reverent prayer for forgiveness; prayer to the Glory of God who, though man is a miserable worm beside him, reaches His hand down and says, 'Work. Increase. Multiply your talents which I have entrusted unto you.'

"The story has a beautiful ending . . . ."

NOTES for the Text circa 1957

". . . the following spring he returned.

You remember those days. War just over. War the second judgment. Men without jobs. People turning from the fold: 1. Divorce. 2. Insanity and drunkenness. 3. Murder, suicide, and whoring. 4. More colleges. More communists and philosophers in colleges.

The third judgment like Plagues of Israel. Recession. Korean War.

Boy returns from Army . . . . Foreman at factory follower.

False prophets—Supreme Court. 1. God divided world into separate dominions. 2. Cain. 3. Holy matrimony = family, destroy children. 4. What equal means.

Almost all of you have families. You know joys of work, raising little ones and bringing them to Christ, tithe and support of missions in Africa, prayer and holy congregation.

The story has a beautiful ending . . . .

NOTES for the Text circa 1967

". . . the following spring he returned.

You remember those days. Russia. Communists. McCarthy dead. Crime.

The fourth judgment. Fear and dissent. Assassination (Kennedy). Cuba. Negroes. Riots. Law doomed and spit on. Protection of criminals. (Hoover attacked by newspapers.)

Boy goes to city. Follower man who eats dope. (Insanity, blood poison, needles, waste away.)

False prophet Buddha—zen—Love everyone (fornication, adultery, venereal disease). No marriage, no heaven, dancing, music, nakedness. (Babylon. Jonah, sons walk backward to hide shame.)

Almost all of you have someone in cities. You know fears of temptation, violence, harlotry, and liquor. Fear evils of irreverence, men who corrupt women (or other men), radicals, and humanists.

And you know the joys of righteousness and gathering together in Holy communion of the Spirit.

The story has a beautiful ending . . . .

NOTE for the Text circa 1977

". . . the following spring he returned."

Play Like I'm Sheriff

Sunset lay behind the tall buildings like red and yellow smoke. The cloud cover was high. Shadows of the buildings fell across the circle that was the business center of downtown Indianapolis. The towering monument to war dead was bizarre against the darkening horizon. On it figures writhed in frozen agony, except when they caught the corner of his eye. Then they seemed to move, reflecting his own pain.

About the circle a thousand people hurried. The winter cold was nondirectional as the circle enclosed the wind and channeled it here and there. The temperature was nearly freezing. Lights in store windows began to glow with attraction and importance. Everywhere there was movement.

He stood before a store window, a young man of slight build with uncut black hair, looking at coats. There was tension about his eyes. Occasionally his mouth moved. Muttering. Then his face would tense under a surge of mental pressure.

The mannequins in the window smiled; tiny female smiles dubbed on faces above plaster breasts and too-narrow legs. Some of the coats were gaily colored. Others were black with fur collars. Some were fur. The wind hailed against his thin work jacket but he was not cold. He was accustomed to weather much harder than the kind blowing.

There was no question in his mind that he was a little insane. He sobbed. Not because he was insane, but because his wife had not ever had a nice coat. Only a few times had she had really nice dresses. He felt a deep and very personal shame. She had come so far with him. He sobbed, trying to divert his thoughts and remembering that he had read that madness was never admitted. He wondered if anyone else had ever admitted it to themselves. He thought of the man who would be his wife's new husband and wondered if he would buy her fine clothes.

Farther down the street he believed there might be another store. He walked slowly, looking. Unhappiness depressed his body so that he walked with a slight stoop. Before he found another store a girl idled along beside him, walking slowly, just fast enough.

"Hello," she said, and smiled a little cleaver of a smile. He was taken by the look of her, but in his mind there was no inventory. He was conscious only of a female image. It was very general. Light and dark hair mixed. A slim girl with a pretty face. He was fooled at first, vaguely wondering if she were lost and wanted direction. The word direction sang in his head and caused him to smile.

"Hello," he told her. He walked at the same pace. She fell in beside him. It seemed almost as if they were going somewhere. As if there was a place to go and something that must be done when they arrived.

She was silent for a little while. "Do you know," she said finally, "I've come from home with practically no money. I could stand a drink. Or a sandwich." Her voice had started softly. It ended strained.

He looked at her. "Come on. It's cold here."

In the half light of the bar she seemed younger and more unhappy. He took time to look, surveying her across the table while he felt in his pocket for the fifteen dollars that must buy restaurant food and bus fare to work for the next four days. He found himself wanting to go home, reacting familiarly with despair as he realized for some thousandth time that it was impossible.

As always with women he was shy. Now he did not know how to tell her. He did not want to miscall her and edged around it.

"I'm pretty broke, myself," he told her. "Will be all this week."

She did not leave. She did not seem disturbed about the money. "I'll pay for the drinks. The money part wasn't true. I have some."

"I don't understand."

She suddenly seemed smaller. Almost like a child. "Talk," she said. Her voice was also smaller. She looked at him as if she were lost. "Talking to. There's lonesome in the wind. I walked to the bus station, and there was lonesome in the crowd. Like something evil hovering . . . I haven't talked to anyone for more than a week."

Her voice, as much as what she said, told him. He looked directly at her. "You're crazy, too. You've found a good ear. A good voice."

"Yes, crazy. I just want to know that someone cares. Cares just something. Want you to know. Want me to know." She hesitated. "You are so unhappy. Look so unhappy. I wouldn't have been able to speak otherwise."

"Maybe no one does care. You said it. There's lonesome all over."

She watched him. Her coat hanging beside the booth was new.

"Norma," he said. "Norma Marie."

"It isn't, but I know what you mean."

A crowd of couples came through the doorway. They were laughing. He watched them then looked at her. "What do they know?" he asked.

"How to pretend," she said. "I don't really like to drink. Let's go."

They walked a long way off the circle to a parking lot. The wind pressed at the back of his legs. The girl wore no hat. Her hair was blowing.

The car was good but not new. She drove it for a long time out of the center of town. He wondered if he was supposed to make love to her, then wondered if he could. Instead of touching her he lit a cigarette and passed it. His hand was trembling.

"No," she said, taking the cigarette. "I don't think so. At least not now." She smiled at him and he felt ashamed, felt himself withdrawing into recollections of another time which held more shame. "I'll do better," he told his wife under his breath. The girl touched his hand.

"Talk," she told him. "Talk away at the lonesome first. Maybe that's all it will be."

"Do you tell me or do I tell you?"

"I don't know." She drove slowly for several minutes. He watched the streets and then the sky where the clouds seemed to be lowering. There was no light except along the streets.

She turned a corner. He realized suddenly that she was also nervous, more than she had been. "My house is down this block," she told him. "I have a whole house."

"You don't even know my name."

"I think it's Johnnie. If it isn't, lie to me."

"You guessed right," he lied. "But I haven't been called that in years." He thought it sounded authentic.

"You lie good," she told him.

"Only to myself."

The house was a tall white frame. The driveway and porch were dark. She parked the car at the back of the drive.

"My grandmother's house," she told him. "Then mother's. Then mine. Any sound will be grandma trying to get out of the attic." She laughed faintly.

"You mean haunted?" He watched her, wondering at her nervousness and at himself. The pressure of his hurt, the tension in his mind, was not relaxed but was relaxing. He quickly pulled the hurt to him because it was his and familiar. "Haunted?" He wondered if she were not worse than himself.

"Sure. Ghosts get as lonesome as people." She tried to smile and it did not work. "At least, I think they must." She stared through the windshield at the sky. "I think it will snow."

She turned to him, the tension seeming to break a little with controlled excitement. "I pretend a lot. Since I was little . . . . Well, for a while I didn't pretend. Yes, I did. But now I pretend a lot. Like when you were little you know, and you said 'Let's play like I'm the sheriff and you don't know I'm here and you come around that corner.' . . ."

"I remember."

"All right. Now, I'll play like Norma and you play like Johnnie and we'll go into our house and I'll fix dinner. And while I fix dinner you can sit in the kitchen and talk. And be friendly. And good, and tell me how well I'm doing, because . . . ." She turned to him. Her eyes held tears that she would not allow to come. "Because he never did, you know."

"But, you pretended." He could not help interest.

"Of course. Didn't you?"

The question alarmed him. He sat watching the sky through the windshield and was quiet for a long time. Finally he turned toward her. "Yes, but I called it lying to myself."

"It is. Do you like the real way better?"

"No." The longing for something that could not be came back hard. He felt it, then fought it, surprising himself. "All right. Pretend." He opened the door on his side and she watched him. He got out, walked in front of the car and around to open the door for her. When she got out it was with a smile that he believed, and not a muscular gesture. "You never did that before," she whispered.

"I will now," he told her. "I will show you more care now, but I'm sorry for before."

"Don't be sorry." She took his hand and they walked around the old house. "People should use their front doors," she told him, "it makes them more important."

The house looked like a museum. The furniture was of mixed periods. He recognized some as old and valuable. There was antique glassware sitting about. The rooms were ordered and neat.

"We are the fourth generation in this house," she said. "It's always good to think that."

"I don't know much about my family," he said truthfully.

"I know," she told him, "but that's not important. As long as we're proud of us."

He took her coat, holding it and looking about.

"Thank you," she said. "The closet under the front stairway will do." She moved from him, through a series of rooms to the back of the house. He hung the coat and his jacket in the closet, which was empty except for an old trench coat. He looked at the coat, thinking it long enough to fit him but made for a heavier man. Then he walked through the rooms where she had gone. He found her working at the counter in the kitchen. The kitchen was modern, contradicting the rest of the house. He stood, not quite knowing what was expected of him. "Can I help you?"

"No," she smiled. "Just sit with me." Her movements at the counter seemed natural and nearly familiar. She looked at him seriously, then hesitated. "I'm glad to have you home." Her voice was faint, but it seemed clearly determined.

He was surprised, then remembered. "I'm glad to be home."

There was a different kind of worry on her face. "I was afraid. Well, you like Charlotte too well. I wish she were married."

He looked at her. "Not that well. A friend."

"Too well, and she's awfully crude."

"Yes," he said. "I wish she would move. Tough. Very hard."

"She's been gone since you left, and I thought."

"Of course. But, here I am."

"Sometimes. Oh, I'm sorry. Sometimes you're hard and I don't understand."

He was startled and then defensive about being charged with something he could never be. "I'll not be that, not anymore. I'm different now, you know. I've stopped losing my temper." He wondered if he were saying right. The girl had her back turned, working rapidly. Then she turned to face him. Her face held shame.

"I'm sorry about something, too. I was going to kill myself if I didn't find you tonight. You'd been gone so long."

He was startled. "How long has it been?"

"Nearly five months. Your mother called last night and said you were on the coast. She wanted the rings back. She wasn't kind." She turned back to work. "How did you get home so soon?"

"I flew." He did not understand his action, but he rose and walked to her. He touched her shoulder.

"Sometimes," she said, "you used to touch me here." She placed his hand in her hair. "It'd be all right if you muss it." He touched gently under and about her hair.

"Thank you," she said, then turned to him with a pretended smile because the hurt was deep in her eyes. "Now go," she told him, "or go hungry."

"I'd rather go hungry."

Her hands shook over the bowl. "Thank you again," she said. He returned to his chair. "Kill yourself?" He wondered, thinking that she was even more troubled than himself. Then he denied it out of an obscure loyalty to his own trouble. He wondered if there were not more complications than he could handle, and he wondered that he cared.

"My grandmother was so happy," she said. "This fine house, fine husband and nice children. But my mother was not. So I locked her in the attic."

"Your mother?"

"No. You know when we buried her. But grandma died when I was little. I helped carry her things to the attic. They told me . . . . I don't know. Whatever you tell children. But she has lived in the attic ever since. But I locked the door. Against losing her, you know."

"But, kill yourself?"

"By going to sleep. In a special way. Someday, and that day was tonight, I think, it would have come on so very lonesome. With you gone. With you gone. And only people to talk to who wanted to buzz at you. Friends, you know." Her back was still turned. He watched her tense, then clench her hands and he heard the bitterness in her voice. Then her hands relaxed a bit. Her voice was low and strained. Worse, he thought, than it had been.

"When no one cares. What to do?"

"What were you going to do?" He was surprised at the softness of his voice.

"Get the key and unlock the door. Then I was going up the steps. Very narrow. Very straight. And I'd go quietly and catch her asleep. And I'd say 'Grandma, grandma,' and she would come, like when I was little . . . . I had a dog once, remember I told you, but he died. That dog loved me. I played with him when I was a little girl. And grandma loved me—and, she'd touch me and hold me and make me like a little girl again, because, because . . . ." Her speech stumbled and the tensions moved to tears and heavy weeping. "Because I'm so damn lousy—at being a woman."

He moved to her quickly around the counter and held her while she wept. She was tense in his arms. Her body seemed slim nearly to thinness. He was confused. Wondering who. Wondering what was her name.

"Norma," he said, and held her closer.

She raised her head to look at him while still weeping. "Do you want me? Will you want me? I'll do so very badly." She lowered her head. "But I'll try. Because I'm crazy now. I'll be lots better crazy."

"Wait," he told her. "Come now, calm down." He felt nearly afraid. "Come, sit down." He moved to try to lead her to a chair.

"No," she told him. "It's all right. It will be all right." She moved back toward him. He smoothed her hair as he held her. They stood for several minutes until her weeping subsided. Then she turned and left, to come back with a handkerchief. She was trying to smile.

"I took my vacation to find you. The whole two weeks."

The continued pretense made him angry. He reacted in a way familiar to him and became very quiet. It occurred to him that she needed him more than he needed her. It was a strange and warm feeling to be needed. Then it occurred to him that he might be lying to himself again.

"I changed jobs." He paused. "The other wasn't that good anyway." A rush of misgiving overcame him. He had surprised himself by having been taken by the pretense. "I wanted to do better."

"Better?"

"Not right away." He heard shame in his voice. "In a little while you get raised."

"Don't worry about money. Oh, please, not now. Don't worry." She turned to the window then turned back with a tiny laugh.

"See," she told him, "I was right. It's snowing."

He stood and went to the window. The snow was light and carried by the wind. "A light fall," he said.

"It will get heavier." She was placing silver and dishes on the table. "I just have wine." Her voice was apologetic.

"Just a little," he told her. She looked up quickly.

"The table looks so pretty," he said.

"Thank you."

"And the house looks nice."

"I kept it for when you came. Now we'll eat before it's cold."

The meal went well. They ate quickly. She seemed more at ease to him. Once or twice the unfamiliarity of his surroundings surprised him. Or he looked at the girl and recoiled at the pretense. When that happened memories of his wife and memories of his loss and aimlessness came back. His mind would try to recede each time into the trouble. Instead, he would speak.

"When I was little," he told her, "we'd watch a snow like this. Kid hungry, you know. If it were early in the year, like tonight, Dad would watch for a while. If it got heavy he'd get the sleds out of the barn. We'd polish the runners."

"Great Grandfather died on a night like this," she told him. "When I was very little. I mostly remembered the snow. I've always loved it. Like a fresh beginning in the morning."

"You've always lived here?"

"Always here." She looked at him reproachfully, maintaining the pretense. "I didn't know you ever lived on a farm. You should have known about Great Grandfather."

"Yes."

She smiled, then stood to clear the table. "But I'll tell you something the cousins never told you. He didn't come to Indiana because of the oil wells. He left Philadelphia in front of a shotgun."

"Girl?"

"The family skeleton. No, that's not kind to say. Because the girl died soon after. I don't know how."

He helped to clear the table while she placed dishes in the sink. "He was an old rip, I guess. But I've always loved the snow."

While she ran water in the sink he moved to help her. She turned, surprised, but said nothing. They worked together quietly.

He stacked the dry dishes on the counter. When the work was done she began putting them away.

"Do you know," she said, "I'm so tired. I seem to get tired quicker, lately."

He watched her. Unsure. "I figured it out because I'm the same way. Every minute you're awake you're tensed up, burning energy. I sleep a lot."

"Good," she said. "Come with me." She took his hand and they walked slowly through the house to ascend the front stairway. At the top of the stairs she hesitated. He stood beside her, moving away a short distance. He did not hold her hand.

"No," she said. "That way is the door to the attic." There was some quality of determination in her voice. She took his hand and led him down a hall to the front bedroom. The room was very dark until she pulled the shades at the front window. Tall trees stood bare before the house, partially obstructing a streetlight. The snow fall was getting heavier. It was still being pushed by the wind.

"Please stand here," she said and squeezed his hand. He stood, watching through the window and listening to her movement about the room.

When she spoke her voice was faint. "You used to like to watch me but I was shy. I still am but not so much."

He stood watching the snow. The onetime familiar feeling of excitement filled him as the snow swirled about the streetlight. When she stepped beside him she was naked to the waist.

"I love you," she said, "I was so stupid to doubt." Her breasts were lighted by the faintness of the snow-shrouded streetlight. They were shadowed underneath. The light fell across her face and hair so that he saw that she was beautiful with the prettiness. Her face seemed even more sensitive than before. Then across her face there seemed a small realization of fear.

"We stood this way once," she murmured.

He nodded, saying nothing, but knowing that with the fear and the pretense he could not make love to her.

"Would you like to sleep now?" he asked.

"Yes." She smiled. The fear vanished as she saw his understanding. "But, first. Hold me, please." He put his arm about her waist then moved to touch her.

"Thank you," he said, and he did not know why.

"Come." She led him to the bed which was on a darkened side of the room. She lay down and he removed his shoes then lay beside her. He did not touch her. They were quiet. He listened to her breathing. It seemed to him that the darkened room was filled with questions and the questions were mostly about himself.

"Norma?"

"Yes."

"Are you still pretending?"

"I'm not sure. In parts, I think."

He paused. "I always blamed myself, you know. Never figured anyone was wrong but me."

He touched her hand. It was relaxed and did not respond. Her breathing was quiet. For a moment he felt badly. "Maybe I was right," he said. "Nobody does care. Maybe nobody cares for anybody."

"Don't," she said. "You're feeling wrong. Not for you they don't care that way. Maybe they don't care. Not for me. But each cares that no one cares for the other."

"That isn't enough, is it?"

"No. That isn't enough. But it's enough to keep yourself from dying. And, thank you."

"My mind gets so full of the other . . . ." He realized what she had said. He tried to draw back a small feeling of pride.

"And mine," she told him. "But can you pretend a thing until it's real?"

"I think it's what we haven't learned." He touched her hand again. This time she held his. "In the morning when we get up I'll say hello to you. I'll say, 'I love you, Norma' and you'll say . . . "

"I'll say, 'I love you, Johnnie.' "

"And I'll go to work."

"If the streets aren't impossible I'll drive you. Then I'll go back to work. And when work is over . . . ." She stopped. He wanted badly to tell her that at least he was really wondering about tomorrow.

"You don't know," he told her instead.

"That's the truth. Yes. That's the truth. I don't. Maybe it's how hard you pretend, Johnnie." She turned to him and whispered her shyness. "Before we sleep, will you pretend something if it doesn't hurt? Will you kiss me and say good night and call me Catherine? Not Cathy, but Catherine. Then I'll pretend for you and call you . . . ."

He held her and kissed her. He was surprised at her response in the short kiss. Her body against his seemed in some way familiar. He did not know if it was the familiarity of the form of Norma who was not there or the familiarity of the stranger who was. There was a rush of pressure in his mind. He had lived with it for so long. Now he fought it back.

"Thank you, Catherine," he told her. "And, something that just occurred. Maybe you have to love yourself a little first, Catherine."

She touched his hair. His hand felt necessary to him against her back. He wondered what his hand meant to her.

"Pretend, Catherine," he whispered gently. "Good night, Catherine," he said.

The Shark

On the steel deck it looked dead until it was kicked. When that happened the dry body would flop. The mouth would fall open, backing into the underbody to display the thousand serrations of needle teeth in banked triple tiers. There was a cut, now baked dry, back of the head. The bone structure of the mouth was punched in one spot where it had been hit with a chisel. A wire ran through the hole replacing the hook. It was bent to a piece of twenty-one thread. The shark was small, about three feet, but in a way it was a record. It had been alive for six hours.

It was Gamper's shark. Its longevity made him proud. He knew that they did not often live long, that like rabbits suffering stroke from a single pellet sting, sharks did not often live much past the catching. Gamper had set himself the task of keeping this shark alive.

He gave the shark a jerk with the line. His face was impassive except at the moment of the jerk, when it held a snarl. "I'll kill this sorry damn thing if it takes all day," he announced generally.

Behind him another man lounged at the rail of the cutter, taking advantage of the shade. The shark lay in the bow, on the sun-heated plates behind a winch. The metal was very hot. A man could not walk about the deck with bare feet. Through a nearby hatch came the desultory sounds of a card game, mingling with the experimental plucking of a guitar.

"Hit me," a voice said. "Stand," the voice said. Then in a conversational tone the voice lifted. "Gamper, how's your fish coming?"

The man standing at the rail stirred. Gamper turned to him, a tough grin on his weathered face that was small and exactly proportioned but not pleasing. "Let's put him back over," he said.

The man, Fernandez, stood without moving. The Gulf of Maine heat that could be dispelled by the slightest breeze lay oppressive about the anchored cutter. Her rail aft was festooned with yellow drying loops of manila line. The line was still damp and steaming from the tow of the broken-down vessel the night before. When the line was dry it would be flaked out on the fantail for the next search and rescue.

"Sunday," a player's voice said. "Last day of patrol. I bet we catch a job and don't get home."

"Don't even think it," another voice warned.

"Bet we do. It happened last five times out of seven. I kept count."

"So, quit counting."

"Bet on something else," a third voice suggested. "Two-bit pot on how long Gamper keeps his fish alive."

"Why not," the second man answered. "Make out twenty minute slips and draw for a quarter." The voices sank to a drone. Fernandez had not moved. Gamper looked at him hard. He gave the line a tug.

"Let's put him back over."

Fernandez attempted a look of dignity and contempt. "You put him over."

"Not alone. He's still got some stuff."

"Then get a gun from Cap and put him out of his misery. You had your fun. Now shoot him."

"Pee on his misery." Gamper twitched the line. The body gave a jerk. "He's still got some stuff. He's not done yet."

"You mean cooked." Fernandez stood up to leave. He was ship steward's mate, the junior man. He had no authority. "You're a big man, Gamper. You're a hero. Put him over yourself, and I hope he takes your arm."

"Don't push it."

"Then kill him. You had your fun." Fernandez stepped through a hatch into the shaded heat of the passageway. He disappeared into what seemed absolute darkness after the glare of the deck and sea. Words from the card game greeted him. He was asked about the execution, twitted about the shark. They suggested to him that if he did not buy it for the wardroom mess the crew would be stuck. The man experimenting with the guitar motioned to him.

"No."

"Sure," the man said. "All you Mex play guitars."

"Texas."

"All right. All you Texans play guitars." The man motioned again. Fernandez sat beside the man to show him a chord. Through the passageway came another flop. Fernandez found the chord and hit it hard.

"That Gamper is a natural damn louse," he said.

A quartermaster looked up. Shark, guitar, and card game had been uninteresting. He was reading a magazine. Now he yawned and stretched like a cat. "Naw," he said. "Gamper ain't any meaner than you. Gamper's scared."

"Scared? It's just a garbage shark. Why scared?"

"All guys are scared of sharks. Gamper's just showing it."

Another thump sounded on deck. Then Gamper's voice said, "Okay, fishy, I'll put you over myself."

A man rose from the table. "This I gotta see. If he's such a hot shark now's the time for him to prove it." He went out. There were several thumps. The card game continued undisturbed. The man who had gone out to observe returned.

"Snugged the line and his head up hard to the rail, threw a bowline around the tail and pitched him over. Like to broke its back, but hell, you can't bust shark bones. Then he unhitched the line and dropped him. Easy."

"What do you mean, scared?" Fernandez asked again. The

quartermaster had resumed his reading. He grunted and did not answer.

"That girl was sure to hell crying." A player picked at a former discussion.

"Well, the other woman was there. Maybe she helped."

"The old guy sure God wasn't her daddy."

"Next time she'll say no to a boat ride. She ain't fresh meat no more."

"What do you mean, scared?" Fernandez asked again. "Garbage sharks don't hurt anyone." The quartermaster stirred, irritated.

"You've seen bodies come up. You've snagged bodies. Well . . . ." He motioned with a thumb to the hatch. "He don't understand."

The men pretended indifference. A silence fell. Occasionally a man asked for a card. The deal passed once, indifferently. Most of the men had seen bodies. They are a part of a Coast Guard's experience, perhaps the worst part. Each man had his own mental picture of how a body comes to the surface, tossed and eyeless as the salt water washes in the scavenged eye sockets. The fingers and toes are gone, along with the lips. If the clothes are torn the soft body parts are gone and the bloat and stink of the body wells out of the holes.

They are lifted out with a wire basket, like a stretcher. The basket is dragged under them with lines. They are netted by the basket because otherwise the body might pull apart. The smell is very bad. Bodies are stored under canvas on the fantail. If it is a really bad one the smell permeates the ship and men get sick. When that happens the cooks keep only coffee going. A few men eat sandwiches as a brag. Scavengers hover over death. If a shark finds a body the body does not rise. The shark is the king of all scavengers. The men had seen various things.

A player stirred, then gave a conscientious chuckle, deliberately trying to break the mood. "Best job I ever heard was a fella evacuated a cat house."

"Naw." Another man forced a grin.

"Sure. Gibbs, seaman. Knew him at the lifeboat station. He had a letter one of the women wrote to the newspaper."

"Why? What did he do to her?"

"Good letter, I mean. A bosun mate and Gibbs were out in a thirty-eight picket. The boats brought it right through a flood to the window of the house. Old Gibbs went in there and started carrying out whores and their stuff in a forty-knot blow. They didn't even think the boat would make it. Brought her in with the spaces looking like a combination cat house and dime store."

"Life and property, man. But he must of made out."

"I reckon later. The girl really branded his tail with that letter. Everybody knew what she was and razzed Gibbs."

"Hey, hey, look at him go!" The players looked at each other, reacting against the edge of hysteric hatred in Gamper's voice.

"That jerk."

"At it again." The quartermaster put down his magazine. "You'd foul up a free lunch, Gamper," he was trying to yell him down. "You'd screw up the Last Supper."

The voice from the deck was a hiss. "It was pretty screwed up without me."

Fernandez stood up. "That flushes it," he said. "I'm getting a gun." He turned and went down a short passage where a ladder led to the bridge.

The quartermaster grinned up. "He's scared too."

"Shut up," a voice said.

The quartermaster grinned. "Have it your way. If there's going to be a shoot-out I think I'll watch." He stepped through the hatch and stood at the rail. The other men looked at each other, played out the hand, then rose and went out on deck.

Looking over the rail they could see the shark plunging hard against the line. He would plunge, he brought up hard, then allow himself to surface gradually, gathering strength for his next hard dive. The heat was intense. The men loosened or took off their shirts. The shark rolled his white belly and dived hard. He was a tough shark.

A voice spoke nervously. "Worst I ever had was one we got two years ago. Worked it off a cutter instead of a boat like we should of. Back must have been busted. He fell right in half. God!"

"Why don't you club him?" a man asked Gamper. "That's the way to kill a shark."

"Don't suffer enough."

Another voice spoke. It was tense. "Worst I ever had wasn't even wet. We were on harbor patrol. This old party waved us in to an island. He was drunk as hell, and four of them had borrowed somebody's island for a weekend tour. Two men, two women, all about fifty or better. Their boat drifted or something. Anyway, this guy says he's got a sick woman, but she wasn't. She was dead as a nit. Sitting at a table, naked and weighing maybe three hundred pounds. When we lifted her there was this real bad look on her face. Bareass dead, man, and looking like she was staring at the center of Hell!" He paused apologetically. "You just don't forget one like that," he said.

A bell sounded inside the cutter.

"Calling the engine room," the voice was a protest. "If it's a job . . . . Who was that jerk that was counting?"

"If it's a job they'll tell us." The quartermaster looked up. The bridge was silent. "Gamper, you better get rid of your shark. If we got a job . . . ."

Fernandez came through the hatch without a gun. "The old man says to club him. He won't give me any gun."

Gamper looked at him. "Was that an order?"

The steward looked as if he wanted to lie. The men's faces told him that they could read him. "No," he said. "But do something. Radio is working one."

"Hell."

"Worst I ever had," another man was beginning eagerly, imposing his story against time, "was blue. He was stealing lead cable from a government island and overloaded and floundered in a White squall. I think it scared him blue, and then he died."

"In the water they change." Gamper pretended interest.

"Naw—this one was fresh. We got the grapple in his left eye, and he was dark blue, shooting out red when he came up. I still dream . . . . The hell with it . . . ."

"Stand back," Gamper announced. "I'm bringing him back up."

He started hauling in on the line. A chief bosun mate came through the hatch. "Story time?" he asked.

"I'll tell you one, chief." The quartermaster grinned.

"I'll tell you one. We got a sinker working. Trawler. The water is getting ahead of his pumps."

"In this calm?" The quartermaster was indignant. "How far off?"

"Some of them things leak in drydock." The chief was grinning at the indignation. "He's five and a half, six hours off."

"Sea's good," another man said. "We ought to get him."

"If the tide change don't bring wind." The chief turned. Gamper had the shark level with the rail. The chief looked at it, then looked at Gamper. "Games," he said. "Bad luck on Sunday. Get rid of it."

"Bad luck to let one go." Gamper was suddenly angry. He bounced the line.

"Depends on how you let it go. You screwed away a whole day with that thing. It takes two minutes. Take a turn in that line, then shag below for some of that scrap from the new shoring. Put a couple nails in." Gamper went.

When he returned, the chief took the nailed-together pieces that looked like a kite frame. He attached a wire to the nails, then with a line hoisted the shark's tail and twisted the wire onto the tail. The frame would drag about two feet behind.

He took a knife from his pocket. "You have to mend this line," he told Gamper. He lifted the tail level with the rail. With the knife he made several fairly deep cuts in the white belly. "Needs to bleed a little," he explained. The blood oozed red and waterish from the cuts. Then the chief let the tail drop so that nothing but the head of the shark appeared beside the rail, the eyes dull, lethargic, and unaccusing. With the precision of a striking gull the chief picked twice with the knife and the eyes popped. The body drummed against the side of the cutter. The chief cut the line and the body fell to the water. The shark dived and tried to swim deep. The blocks floated just below the water's surface.

Gamper checked his watch. "Made it a little over seven hours, anyway," he said to no one.

"Might make it for a couple more," the chief said. "The little fish will eat out his belly. Now you deadbeats get to work." He turned and went forward to where the anchor detail was assembling. There was a rumble, and the stack belched black, then the engine settled to a steady throb. "Power on the winch?" he asked.

"We got it, chief." The winch began to make turns. There was the slow rattle of chain in the hawsepipe. The sun was very hot. The anchor detail wiped sweat and cursed the hot deck. The cook stuck his head through the hatch and told Fernandez to make fresh coffee. Fernandez stood as if he did not hear. He stared after the chief.

"Sea's good," the quartermaster said to no one in particular. He started to walk forward to the bridge ladder, then hesitated. A puff of air was faint, it might have been the ship moving now that the anchor had broken ground. The quartermaster sniffed at the air with the studied, judicious manner of a man privy to bridge secrets.

"Sea's good," he repeated. "Awful good . . . don't know what that jar-head means. This tide won't bring no change."

The Sounds of Silence

Donizetti is dead. Louis Armstrong is dead. Vancouver is another rainy city.

Velma Middleton is dead. Mozart. J. B. Arban. Stravinsky. The ranks form in my mind. Composers, performers, all of them teachers. I stare into the rainy streets at a store front which advertises cheap boots. Galli-Curci is dead. The water pounds like nails. Jim is walking around out there someplace.

The theme does not leave my mind and I do not try to dislodge it. The Firebird. The horns and trumpets have it on open bell and the music is wild and triumphant. We came to this motel a half hour ago, a fifty-year-old man with thinning hair and his nineteen-year-old son. How many journeys? How many miles? It has only been a few hours.

Jim's guitar is in the corner and his trumpet is by the bed. On my next visit I'll bring the cello. For the last hour all of my memories have seemed less than one morning old.

Because it is not yet noon. We left Seattle early. Jim slowed toward the end of the packing. He was discarding books and folding things that did not need to be folded. Always before the room was cluttered, the evidence of rebellious sloppiness never quite hidden. His mother and I have tried for order in our lives and have been successful. Jim will use those learned patterns later.

He is a tall kid. This morning he was learning to become a man and he slumped under his decision. We had talked it out on an evening last week. After the defensiveness and flamboyance and third-world metaphor, his decision (stated quietly and almost with surprise) was a relief. He would refuse the draft. He would go to Canada.

I hope I did well. Finally, even between husband and wife, father and son, there is a vacuum that cannot be bridged and I believe it is the first part of maturity to recognize this. I also believe it is the first part of wisdom to continually struggle against it.

Jim's new haircut is too short. He looked like a Marine home from boot camp. Last summer's tan ran halfway up his forehead to a demarcation where the hair had thickened and curled, sometimes falling nearly to his eyes. His eyes are blue, touching toward green like his mother's. He had been proud of his hair. I felt sentimental and then did not feel that way. What are these symbols? He could grow his hair down his back once we got into Canada.

"I'll bring those," I said. He stood with a half dozen phonograph records and a puzzled look.

"Now?"

"When I come up next time." His walls were covered with posters. It would be necessary for me to come back and clean the room. "Will you want these?" I motioned to them.

"No." He laid the recordings on the single bed and stared from a window. Short answers were all he had on tap. Over the past years the posters had changed. When he was a freshman he surrounded himself with hatred. Clenched fists, gutter words, lampooning and sarcastic statements. Now the hatred seemed temporarily stilled, either by mental fatigue or a change of perspective. I hoped for change. Of all things I feared, the hatred was the worst.

In a way he was already a veteran. He has been beaten twice, once by a policeman and once by a carload of drunks who caught him on the street late at night. The posters were of trees and beaches and birds. I wondered if he really watched those things. I did not at nineteen, and now I doubted that Jim did either.

"About ready?" It is hard to make your voice kind. Your intention clouds the natural kindness.

"You go ahead. I'll be right down." His voice was harsh.

It was good-bye to a particular place and it seemed strange to me that he was learning this. Both my wife and I are musicians. We've said good-bye to a lot of places and felt sad; and some of those places were not as good as this. I turned from the small room in the off-campus house and descended the old stairs. The station wagon, which I trade every three years and which has become a symbol of suburban America, had the seats kicked down and was loaded with suitcases and paraphernalia. It is an expensive car and an indulgence. For so many years I had to own junk, nurse it along, be grateful to a piece of machinery because it did not break down when I could not afford to fix it. Jim scoffs, but I remember. Money went for other things. From the very first lesson he played on instruments of concert quality. You build with good tools.

Already the fog was lifting and commuter traffic was in the streets, taillights popping above the mist-slickened pavement with short darts of brilliance. Traffic lights shifted and clicked, the one at the corner buzzing and stacatto like a small computer. The sky was lowered by the fog and the buildings of Seattle's university district were sharply halved as they disappeared into the overcast. This gloomy place. We have lived here for five years and it suddenly seemed time to go. Perpetually clouded beauty is as difficult to live with as ugliness.

Two girls walked past chattering. Their hair was long and casually tied. Jeans, light jackets, notebooks held carelessly. They were headed for restaurant coffee and an early morning class. Was Jim saying good-bye to his bed? He is respectful of most other people. Even with little experience he will care for his women. I started the car and in a couple of minutes he joined me. His face was set like cast metal. The anger and hatred that I had not seen for a while was back. His sneer was so tight that his teeth showed. It was a wrong way to say good-bye. He climbed in the car.

"Is there anything else?"

"Nope." His voice was telling me that he hated me, the university, the chauvinistic super-establishment; and that, child-like, he was asking for help and getting none. He did not realize that for this there was no help.

Sometimes you talk. Sometimes you listen. Sometimes you shut up. I pulled into traffic, waited for a light, and in five minutes we were on interstate and headed north. If there is pain in living there are also lessons. One does not file as a Conscientious Objector and believe that indignation and good intent are sufficient. During the last part of the interview he was pushed so hard that he yelled manifestos at the draft board.

During the second war the decisions were different but I do not think the men were essentially different. How to explain? I turned the radio on for the noise. There was a lot of it. Pop clanged like untuned cow bells.

Then news. We were still at war.

Then rock, with a perenially breathless, thrust-throated D.J. Jim turned the radio off, perhaps as a concession to me, perhaps for himself.

I looked at him and thought of his mother who does not need to be told that evil exists. She, who reaches beyond the usual perceptions to particularly translate her genius and the genius of others. I have seen two thousand people hang breathless on the spaces between the perfecting and visual strokes of her interpreting bow. She, tall and auburn haired. Happily laughing. A master who teaches a discipline of music so strict that it is transcendental.

"About two hours," I said. "We'll take it easy."

No answer. I think he will begin work now. It has been sporadic. Like poetry, music makes nothing happen. His legs are so long that he propped them against the dash. It dents the padding and makes it crack. I've told him before. This time I did not tell him.

I remembered and must remember. His mother comes from a small town in Wisconsin. The town had no standard of excellence but her teachers did. We met in Baltimore in forty-six at the conservatory. I had just lost four years with the Army. There was a choice for me. My own father's business had leap-frogged during the war. My embochure was gone, my ear no longer trained, and the manual dexterity was imprecise. A French horn operates in four octaves. At first I worked mostly in two of them for six, eight, sometimes more than that hours a day. She was impressed and did not ask why, although from someone else it would have been a good question.

It is a good question now. I could answer it now.

But what would the answer mean to Jim, this passionate American who is committed to a nebulous notion of change in a world that is changing so fast that the young cannot keep up while still believing that they must. After the war there were greater decisions. I do not want to explain. Only this, that in the middle of chaos a man may still concern himself with beauty.

I drove and the speed kept easing upward. That also is an American pattern. Jim rushes everywhere.

After a half hour of driving a thin rain started. It rarely rains very hard in the Northwest. The interstate runs through a variety of land forms and the expressions of towns. Lumber processing plants, knobs, pasture land, high countryside not even good for grazing. To the east are mountains. West lies the sea. It is always green and the interstate runs black and gray between great trees, smokestacks, small businesses whose owners are living out of the till. More fish are dying. More people are dying.

More people are also living.

"You heard nothing this week?" I referred to his inquiry at a Canadian university.

"They hate Americans."

"The university is under-enrolled. I think it will be okay."

"I think so too." He wanted to be friendly and did not do well. "I guess they'll wait until the last minute just to sweat me."

"Paperwork takes time." I thought not of Canada but of this country and sent an imaginary note to a mythical heaven. Dear Sir, when you instituted the New Deal did you realize how dangerous a bureaucracy could become?

The most horrible vision that my mind ever conceived was of my son holding a brick and screaming, his open mouth a fury of hate, his eyes blind with ignorance.

Hey Jude, Hey Jude . . . . I am critical of one thing with these kids. They do not listen to their own music, really listen. Try asking any of them to write down all the lyrics to any popular song.

How can you explain? There are so many great moments. *Universal Judgment.* The bass rumbles in my mind. Would Jim understand if I told him that I once saw Krupa run a syncopation with both feet, tight roll with the right hand, and flipping the stick in the left high over his head to come down with rim shots; in blue light and cigarette smoke, to a lounge filled with sophisticates who were not listening. When I was Jim's age I also played a frumpet.

There was nothing to say. I wondered if my insistence had been too great. In the beginning the practice. Later, the discipline. After an hour of driving I wanted coffee. The road is wide and too straight. It lulls the mind with a false tranquility. Jim was terribly tense. He was startled when I eased down for an exit.

"Trouble," he asked.

"I just want to take a break."

"I can drive."

"If you want." He would not be driving for a long time. He would be studying, if the school accepted him, and also working at a job. Political theory and pumping gasoline, probably. Pumping gas in a world where there is Aaron Copland.

It is hard to think of Jim walking washed-gray Vancouver streets; sleet in winter, automobiles firing through French and English marked intersections like corks popped from bottles. He is correct in some respects. He will not always be welcome, not if he is only another displaced American. He will have to work hard.

I found a restaurant and parked. The place seemed a monument to plastic and luminescent paintings on black velvet. A construction crew sat in one booth, the men with strong shoulders and weather-beaten faces. Eloquent hands and eyes. I have seen workmen in this country hit the fine line on a grade using little more than a bulldozer. In Europe they would use grading rakes and take a week. The crew did not know that they were improbable people, only that their competence was assumed. Jim almost certainly filed them in the category "hard hat" and took a seat at the opposite end of the room. He sat facing them. It was not easy to watch him finding strength in hatred. With the fresh haircut he seemed nearly hatchet-faced. His youth dissolved the impression while his intolerance increased it.

"You're going to have to do better than that," I told him.

"What?"

"You don't know their politics."

"Coke," he told the waitress. I ordered coffee. Jim watched her move away. Young girl.

"It's not the politics, it's a whole rotten value system." He stopped, apparently resolved not to end in dialectics. His face worked to control his hate. Then he was sanctimonious. "They're victims." He tried to smile.

Outside a truckload of new automobiles roared into the parking lot. Plastic ferns in a plastic pot sat by the doorway. The waitress returned with our order. A cash register purred and spit electrically.

"It's not the end of the world," he told me, telling himself.

I agreed and said nothing more. It was the end of one of his worlds. He will never be the same. The flame of his own country's hatred may follow him for the rest of his life. The possibility of being better is the only one he can afford to consider. The coffee was tasteless. I handed him the car keys.

He drove. Jim has always told me what he thinks. He has never asked what I think.

I think that I once carried a rifle and that the business of an army is to take and hold ground.

I am proud of my son and I know that he wants to know that, but he does not know how to ask and I do not know how to tell him. He is both theoretical and ignorant. To one without historical sense explanation means excuse. It increases hatred.

My generation had few philosophers. It came from small towns and cold beds, hell-shouting preachers, petrified morality and depression. After a global war it was a generation concerned with never having to live that way again. My short-haired revolutionary is not a revolutionary at all. We were. He is an exponent of the new Reformation.

"Half an hour," he said, and I was surprised. Thinking. Time was lost, but time to say what?

"You'll do well," I told him. "In a few years the C.O.'s will be repatriated."

"To this God-damned place?" His lips were white and thin.

I stepped on my anger, the anger which he has never asked about. It is a question not of government but of morality in transition. The old is gone, the new not yet arrived, and the average man finds himself more immoral than usual. There are many people who will harm my son. He harms himself.

"A government is not a nation." He is going to find that out, but does not know it now. If there are illusions perhaps it is best that they be kept until he gains strength.

"It all stinks." The tension was so great that his temples were bloodless.

"Have it your way." I wanted to remind him of the many hours of his own practice, remind him of the magic time when the instrument is no longer a problem but an extension. This kid has an instrumental voice that sings, one that needs only authority, and there is no authority in hatred.

His great grandfather was a bugler who played the cornet in the evenings to his troop's horses.

"I just want to get out. I can handle it all, but I just want to get out."

He was defending with hate. Argument was wrong. When we reached the border I leaned back in the seat and stayed silent. There are no guards. It is an open road to Canada, a road easy to plug but I do not think the government wants it plugged. A way to alleviate dissent is to allow it to leave. In less than a mile, past the monument to friendship between two nations, Canadian customs lay in a low-sprawling building with roofs like wings over the road lanes. Jim parked the car. We entered. It was there that inquiries had to be made.

Jim was nervous to the point of trembling. Behind counters men in the uniform of another country were busy. The one who approached us was muscular with a florid face, washed blue eyes, and a conservative and untrained smile. He looked at me, carefully looked at Jim, and guessed the obvious.

"Political asylum?"

It sounded like a spy movie. It sounded unreal.

There were forms. There were questions, places to apply, procedures. It took a long time. Jim was allowed in on a point basis and my function was past. Finally, I did not even function as one who reassures. When I became unnecessary I sat on a bench and waited. Jim talked. The officer talked, called questions to another officer, turned again to speak to Jim. I thought of a ten-year-old awkwardly wrapped around a cello and knew that it was a specifically wrong and stupid thing to do.

The interview ended. Jim turned. We were free to go. Free to find a room, make applications, plot directions toward a continual and, at this time, provisional standard of success.

Jim turned back. His shoulders were hunched with tension. Thin, like a tall child. The officer pointed and Jim walked to an alcove where there were restrooms.

I stood automatically, took one step, waved pointlessly and like a fool to the officers, then reversed my direction and walked outside to the car. His guitar was on top of the load. I pulled it out, the music already beginning like a thin, strong exclamation in my mind.

It's to his credit that there was no sound. Even outside, waiting, I know that there was no sound. He took his time because he had to, and I wondered, holding the guitar and not chording it, if he thought of my unfair anger at some of his practice, at his reasonable foibles. It is certain he thought of his mother, and because of her he thought of the music.

Later, when the control was back, he joined me with swollen eyes that he desperately tried to hide. His mouth was firm, his face and body set in determined lines, and I searched with the certainty of a man who feels the discovery of truth just beneath his fingertips. It was then that the theme burst like a flood in my mind, the sound growing and growing. The brass was walking full. It was strong and proud and victorious.

The Art of a Lady

We kept Uncle George alive during the summer of thirty-two by asking him how was business, which in his case and despite the depression, was excellent. About Miss Chloe Johansen we stopped asking. It would have been as tactful as inquiring of Lady Macbeth if something was bugging her.

Unc was thirty-two in thirty-two, having hit the world at the turn of the century when social stability was beginning to be regarded as a hazard. It worked out perfectly in his case—the whole philosophy, I mean.

He was fair-haired, tall and kind of skinny. Friends wavered over his looks which were between reflective and confused, although Chloe's drinking uncle, Willie, described him as 'Deeper than a gallon.' Despite the increasing dabs at his freedom by the dedicated Chloe (he had given the engagement ring, she kept up the payments) he remained a bachelor.

His main persuasion was that of an artist. Not a paint artist, but a carver of wood. Even though I was only a kid I knew that he was the best carver outside of the Orient, and is to this day. He could whip off a horse for a merry-go-round, shape down the reeds for a bassoon, or do your portrait in the grain of your choice. He did one of Pop in mahogany one time that caused a family scandal. The color of the wood got to him and he made the old man's nose a little flat. Nobody had ever noticed the resemblance before.

But that was his only venture to impressionism if you discount Chloe and Geraldine.

Chloe was just fine. She wanted the same thing other girls wanted, which Unc thought was a glad and good attitude, but she also wanted a wedding band.

Unc would look at her departing form as she moved down the road from his store and hum around in 'Die Valkyrie.'

I'd mutter "Freedom." Unc would take a hitch in his belt and another look, then pat my head.

"Yeh," he would say. Sadly though. Very sad.

He was right. Chloe had a great deal of everything. Geraldine, Chloe's sister, also swung. With her it was mostly mental. She was twenty-eight and had the intellectual nudge on Chloe as well as on the rest of the town. Willie was also her drinking uncle. She claimed to understand Willie. But, while she was intelligent and pretty it was just not in the grand manner so she had plenty of time to think. It was whispered that she thought about Unc.

Reality got them all in trouble. Mostly reality got to Uncle George. When he decided to do a piece of work he did it with the absolute conviction that he would fail. It was a part of his philosophy, one in which many great artists are trapped. He wanted to duplicate experience and nature. He wanted to show exactly how and what a thing was. If he carved a horse—I mean real horse, not merry-go-round, he wanted to be able to sit that horse beside a real horse and let you guess which one was breathing. About half the time you would guess wrong, but Unc always believed you were humoring him. Perfection was his long suit and perfection is what crossed him up in the big 'Figurehead order,' as it came to be known.

Like all artists: painters, writers, perhaps even musicians and acrobats, Uncle George thought of the passing of sail as a loss to part of the soul of man. Being from small town Indiana, he had only a passing notion of what constituted a seaworthy vessel or of the practicality and beauty of a steamship. He just knew sails were beautiful and smoke was not. Also, in the time of sail woodcarvers were in their heyday. Perhaps that had something to do with the figurehead compulsion because he did not really know much about the sea. His only experience with water was the lake where we fished, which on a stormy night would whip up a trough of maybe an inch and a half.

He had a picture book of ship's figureheads that I used to hook while he was at the store, mostly because there were three of the figureheads who (or which) were ladies who (or which) were undressed on top. Uncovered tops were interesting to me. These were well done. Later, when I arrived at high school age I remember being vaguely disappointed.

Chloe and the month of April were surrounding the store at the start of the trouble. Unc had a little house on the highway where he sold antiques, old magazines, his carving and pottery by Geraldine and Chloe who were part-time instructors of the 4H Club. The pottery was splotchy jugs, vases and decorated souvenirs of Hereford City, Indiana. People who had never heard of Rorschach tests became uneasy. Most of the antiques were not really antique, just old. It seldom mattered. Nearly everyone who came in bought something, usually carvings by Unc or pottery by Geraldine which had the most brilliant splotches of all. I guess Uncle George grossed as high as fifteen dollars most weeks, and it was clear profit since he closed at dark. Taxes on the place were a dollar sixty-three cents a year. He did a fair mail order business with regular customers and worked at finished and rough carpentry around the county. I judge he made as high as three thousand in most years. That was good business then. In terms of what it would buy he was no pooch of a marriage prospect.

I was at the store with Chloe and Unc when the Duesenberg pulled up. It was a beautiful car, painted a lovely money-color green. The youngish looking man and woman who got out and traipsed up the path were obviously accustomed to having doors opened for them, so George did. Later, he said he should have locked it.

Entering the tiny, over-stuffed house, the lady tripped over a replica of Doc Sams' prize Poland sow. She staggered here and there, then sat down with a pretty good bump for one so apparently frail. She ended up looking the sow in the face and letting out a fetching scream. I told you Unc had realism cold.

The greasy-haired little guy who was dressed like a house pet and who, we learned later, was a house pet, cursed and kicked the sow in the snoot, chipping it a trifle. He nearly chipped his meal ticket at the same time. To make up for it maybe, he started to threaten a lawsuit. She shut him up pretty quick.

"This man is an artiste," she said, in a phony, rhubarby way that hit Chloe fairly stiff. There was a kind of threat mixed with the rhubarb, even while the lady was still on her can facing the sow. Chloe held herself in, but her blue eyes were hot and she mixed up her blonde hair trying to get it smooth. Who could blame her? She was twenty-three and had given her best years to Unc, the way she figured. She meant in waiting, of course. Maybe it occurred to her that she had never called Unc an 'artiste.'

"An artiste," the lady smiled as George gave her a hand up. She half-whispered to him, asking if he had ever done a self-portrait.

Chloe looked about the way Delilah would have looked if someone told her that on his way over, Samson had been scalped.

After a lot of bazazz from the little rich lady Unc sold the sow on discount because it had a chipped snoot. He also sold a small carving of Chloe's drinking uncle who was his best friend. Willie was county judge and town drunk, held both offices. After two successes, Unc tried to get the lady interested in his impression of an ill duck which looked exactly like an ill duck.

It was just then that the gigolo rolled his eyes and smacked his hand to his forehead so hard he staggered.

"Godiva," he yelled, "he can do Godiva!" Everyone stopped what they were doing to admire the performance. The little woman smiled and nodded.

He had bought her a one hundred-ninety foot schooner to celebrate their great love. Her money, of course, but it was the thought that counted. The vessel had been a bargain. It was the last important thing left from an ex-millionaire's estate who had engaged in 1929 sky diving.

Deceased must have been as bad at seamanship as he was at margins. Before the big crash he had worked up a pretty monumental one of his own. Coming alongside he moved the port of Boston as much as three inches out of line when he hit the entire town. They had the schooner Exchange in drydock for major repairs including bowsprit and figurehead. The plan was to re-name her Godiva II. Unc was courteous enough not to ask who was Godiva I. The old figurehead would not have been fitting anyway. It had been of a broker in a derby hat.

While Unc loaded the chipped sow in the back seat of the Duesenberg (it was a chore, but as he said later, you could get by with almost anything in the back seat of a Duesenberg), the lady bargained with Chloe who had snapped up the role of agent. They agreed on a commission figure of five hundred dollars, two hundred of which the lady paid along with eleven thirty-five for her pig and a buck, six-bits for Willie. Willie, the original, later demanded a snort for modeling. George bought him a tub-full.

Chloe was sharp. Unc would have done the job for thirty dollars. He did not realize the value of art. Most artists never do until they bump someone like Cecil B. DeMille. It was not until the pig was loaded that the situation began to fester.

"Five hundred!" Unc yelled, almost silly happy.

The lady looked worried. "You can do it?"

He watched her as if in devout belief that there would always be a gold standard. She took it for devotion, that was clear. "For five hundred I'd . . . ." He was thrashing around in his head for ultimates.

The lady looked pleased and thoughtful. "You would?"

Chloe interrupted and tried to raise the price.

Then it occurred to Unc that any yacht named Godiva had to have a figurehead that would put the front end of a Rolls to shame. A little hesitancy flickered across his face. The guy and woman insisted on a full-length woman, nude to the waist. The lady insinuated coyly that it might not hurt if the figure wore a satisfied smile. The guy kept looking at Chloe, stating that a very substantial type model should be used. Chloe blushed and kept trying to stop up my ears.

They left it at that. The lady and her escort eventually arrived in Boston and started writing letters to Uncle George.

The first was from the man with specifications for length and mounting. Unc did not allow anyone to read the next letter which was from the lady. He started to walk around with a worried look. Whatever was in the letter could have made little difference because trouble happened before their car had disappeared.

Unc had to have a bare model. You can joke about it now, but in thirty-two in small-town Indiana; or now when I think of it, the prospect of a nude would have caused a riot, a church burning and a jail delivery.

If Unc had been a normal man he could probably have done the job from memory. I mean he was pretty grown-up and had once visited a relative in Indianapolis for a week.

But he was not normal. When he did doc's sow he borrowed the sow. When he carved the duck he had given it a good kick first and then worked like stink before it died, but *that* part had been unforeseen and unfortunate. If he was going to do a nude woman he had to have a nude woman. He was in a bind. As always when in doubt he sought out Willie.

"Marry Chloe," Willie said, tipping the jug. "Art is the iron wrought from the hot forge of suffering." I had tagged along to the courthouse with Unc who packed a prohibition quart. Willie leaned back grinning at the flaking walls of his courtroom. He looked a little flaky himself. Willie was a middling large man with scraggy gray hair and more than a wink for the law. He was also a philosopher, especially with the quart sitting on the bench.

"That's a helluva sentence," I told him. Unc said nothing but I knew I would catch a word or two about that 'helluva' later.

Willie slowly waggled a finger. "Art," he said seriously.

"Art?" Unc said.

"Art," Willie repeated.

"My masterpiece," Unc murmured.

"Freedom," I said. "From every mountain top, let . . . ."

"Go home," Willie told me. "Have another snort of your whiskey, George."

Unc had several. Then he and Willie went to the pool room and talked. There were a lot of people around. I guess that explains how Chloe found out.

The short, sharp and nasty little brawl that developed took place at our house when Chloe stormed in after Unc. I am not sure what had her most angry. It seemed to be the idea of getting her man because he needed to see her naked which is maybe the whole point anyway. But it may have been the idea, as she said, "Of parading my everything over seven seas for every porpoise and dockhand to admire." Chloe could be quite conceited at times.

Whatever the reason she threw the ring at him, then remembered that she had made most of the payments and grabbed it back. She never married Unc although she tried to make him suffer. That succeeded for about two hours until further developments slugged him. The same day another letter came from the rich lady. Three weeks later Chloe was holding hands with one of the Rileys. The turkey growing Rileys, I mean. Not the dirt farmers. Geraldine split her time between the store and Willie's courtroom.

Uncle George was heartbroken but he went back to work. All summer he turned out figureheads that looked like wadded burlesque handbills. They would not have startled your grandmother. I think he finally jointed arms on the whole lot and jobbed them to Si Hansen for scarecrows. It was then that Geraldine came strongly to his aid. The sewing circle started whispering that she had always been a willful child.

Geraldine was always so pretty and so kind. I was nine and planned to marry her myself if she would only wait, even if she was on the rail-skinny side.

She was nearly as tall as Unc with beautiful brown hair and a good eye. But, like I told you she was twenty-eight and an old maid. She must have suffered for Unc a good deal that summer, because finally, as autumn rolled in, she slipped down to the store with her heart in her mouth and her hand on her zipper. It had good results. Unc went enthusiastically to work, sometimes late at night with the blinds pulled. I went catfishing and pondered.

Chloe could never have gone to the store at night, but even the sewing circle was not about to lock horns with Geraldine. Everyone makes at least one mistake in their life and Geraldine had that real good eye . . . .

When the work was done Unc was wearing a sort af dazed look. He decided to deliver the figurehead to dockside himself. He had thrown away none of the rich lady's letters.

He packed the figurehead in Willie's casket without showing it to anyone, then took a train to Boston. The casket was a demonstrator Willie had picked up in 1925, figuring to need it sooner or later. He could never pass a bargain which is the reason it was lent. In payment for its use Unc promised to install a built-in bar.

Despite the letters Geraldine did not protest his leaving. She showed neither doubt nor hesitation. When I asked her what she thought she smiled and said, "Lots."

Everyone else thought exactly what they pleased which was not a little. Geraldine was not fretful. No letters came for her, but she kept busy pricing yard goods and occasionally slipping Willie wet goods. About December she took to hanging around the courtroom. Lectures on philosophy, maybe.

Unc was gone until the following January when he pulled in with the coffin bolted to an old truck chassis. It looked sort of avant-garde and was. He later realized that he had invented the trucking industry's sleeper cab and with it made a fortune.

It was late Saturday morning. I was the only one to meet him. He whirled me around, set me back on the ground and headed for the house. I pried up the lid of the coffin and there was his figurehead dressed in a real bathing suit and a satisfied smile. It was too many for me. I headed for Chloe and Geraldine's house and hid behind the woodpile.

As soon as Unc cleaned up he rushed over. Chloe met him at the door waving a fresh engagement ring.

"Ha," she said.

"Ha, hell," he told her, real frantic, "where's Geraldine?"

She arched a little, pouting, and said that she didn't know. Unc hollered around for a while fairly desperate, then began to believe her.

"Pete Riley," she flourished the ring.

"Really," he seemed interested, "short fellow, dark hair, talks nice?"

"Him exactly."

"How 'bout that?" He dug around for his billfold, opened it and shook his head sadly. "You didn't get any rebate on the other one?"

Chloe disappeared inside the house to come back with a hot stove lid. By that time Unc was on his way to town.

I took a shortcut and made it to the courthouse ahead of him where I ducked behind the rail of the jury box. Unc and Willie adjourned to the courtroom.

"What happened?" Willie breathed into an empty glass and pulled out a shirttail, giving the glass a high polish.

"Where's Geraldine," Unc wanted to know. He leaned forward, scarey-like.

"Get my letter?" Willie breathed at him over the rim.

"I'll . . . . Why did she do it? Leaving with a poet . . . . I'll!" Unc was screaming.

"Easy," Willie told him. "She didn't. I lied. You figure you're the only one with the license?"

"You drunk?" George was stumped. "License to what? Drink?"

"Lie."

"Oh."

"You need a drink."

"Not now, Willie. Where is she?"

"Where she's been all along. Right here in town, be home if there isn't some errand." I figured Geraldine had finally gotten a price on yard goods.

Willie poured one reverently. "What happened," he came at Unc again.

Unc looked worried. "Nothing I'll tell. Well, no, one thing. Godiva II got back to sea."

"With your figurehead?"

"Not the one I took, another one. My masterpiece—I brought the first one back."

"You need a drink."

"No! Now Willie, dammit," he paused sort of uncertain. "I've been busy and I kind of quit." He said it and said it meek.

Willie gave a real horrible laugh followed by a giggle. "Didn't need to," he told Unc. "All you had to do was grease your hair and buy cake-eater shoes."

Unc jumped halfway up. "It's okay," Willie settled him, "I need a drink. You're okay, George, you're okay. Who is on Godiva II?"

"Emma . . . . Uh, the rich lady." And, he said that meek too.

Willie leaned back in his chair gasping with laughter. "Couldn't put her on the bow, huh? Had to go all the way to Boston to trip over yourself."

"Ah, George," Willie waggled his head philosophically, "you're a product of the time. Love one woman while you're with another . . . don't realize it 'til you find you can't flaunt the first one. Whyn't you borrow a swimsuit?"

Inside the jury box I doubled up biting my fists. Unc stood up yelling horrible, kicked the chair from under Willie and took off. Willie lay for a while looking thoughtful. "Puck," he said, "dusted em both, by God." He reached to pull the bottle down for company. By that time I judge Unc had found Geraldine.

They were married in less than three weeks which pleased several old ladies. It gave them something to talk about. They were disappointed at the sewing circle. *Cousin* George did not arrive for two years and *Uncle* George used to stop the busybodies in the middle of the square on Saturday night. He would introduce Cousin George to them as the baby Geraldine carried for twenty-four months. My cousin took after his parents for skinniness and grew up a copy of the rail-splitting Lincoln. He never made it as far as politics, being side-tracked by the wholesale fertilizer business.

What happened in Boston was anybody's guess for a long time. Unc told everyone that the rich lady had given her boyfriend some money and a from-behind kick in the right direction. Everyone theorized that Unc was the replacement but it could not be proved. Since Willie elected to keep quiet I figured it was splendid judgment if I did the same.

However, I did find a notice from a Boston paper in Unc's luggage which told about the unveiling of the figurehead in the rich lady's honor. It was at the time of the official renaming and return from drydock. There was an apologetic reference to some kind of disturbance that was in language I later learned was used in Boston to describe a riot. They have a different way of handling sportive material up there.

The mystery remained for a while and then was forgotten. It was only by chance that I learned a little more some ten years later when Godiva II's captain at the time of the refit came through town on his way west. He was retiring and looking for a little patch of desert or whatever retired captains are chasing. Perhaps because he was getting older, or because he knew no one to the westward, he stopped to have a drink and a yarn with Unc.

I was pretty well grown then, sitting on the porch beside them while the captain had a cold one and settled himself deep in a rocker. They chewed over old times for a while, then talked about the rich lady who had married a Portugese Admiral. Presently the captain eased a look at Unc and said, "George, I'll never understand an artist. There you were with a death grip on two and a half, maybe three million dollars and you settled for a bust on the head with a bottle that knocked you off the platform. You passed, George, you just plain passed. I know you could have married that woman."

Uncle George allowed that it was probably true. In the house Geraldine was singing and Unc just kind of eased back and hummed along on the same tune.

"It's your cussed persistence for exactness did it, George," the captain said. "I'm sorry I've got to say it, but it is. You fouled up Godiva II. You really did."

"Reality," said Unc, breaking into his own humming. "Art is the evocation of reality."

The captain worked that one around pretty sad-like. While he did he knocked off another cold one.

Finally, he said, sort of lumpy and dreamy, "the soul of a schooner is like the soul of a little bird. Under the weight of its own wings it soars, but the soul of Godiva II is dead."

He paused, as if studying for a soft way to say something and hawed around for a little bit, then must have decided to heck with it. "I know you did your best," he told Unc, "but my hand to heaven (and he lifted it) you hurt her best by at least three knots and her feeling of joy. We'd get her offshore with a fair wind and following sea . . . . I'll swear to you George, she just kind of sagged."

Ride the Thunder

A lot of people who claim not to believe in ghosts will not drive 150 above Mount Vernon. They are wrong. There is nothing there. Nothing with eyes gleaming from the roadside, or flickering as it smoothly glides not quite discernible along the fence rows. I know. I pull it now, although the Lexington route is better with the new sections of interstate. I do it because it feels good to know that the going-to-hell old road that carried so many billion tons of trucking is once more clean. The macabre presence that surrounded the road is gone, perhaps fleeing back into smoky valleys in some lost part of the Blue Ridge where haunted fires are said to gleam in great tribal circles and the forest is so thick that no man can make his way through.

Whatever, the road is clean. It can fall into respectable decay under the wheels of farmers bumbling along at 35 in their '53 Chevies.

Or have you driven Kentucky? Have you driven that land that was known as a dark and bloody ground? Because, otherwise you will not know about the mystery that sometimes surrounds those hills, where a mist edges the distant mountain ridges like a memory.

And, you will not know about Joe Indian who used to ride those hills like a curse, booming down out of Indiana or Southern Illinois and bound to Knoxville in an old B-61 that was only running because it was a Mack.

You would see the rig first on 150 around Vincennes in Indiana. Or below Louisville on 64, crying its stuttering wail into the wind and lightning of a river valley storm as it ran under the darkness of electricity-charged air. A picture of desolation riding a road between battered fields, the exhaust shooting coal into the fluttering white load that looked like windswept rags. Joe hauled turkeys. Always turkeys and always white ones. When he was downgrade he rode them at seventy plus. Uphill he rode them at whatever speed the Mack would fetch.

That part was all right. Anyone who has pulled poultry will tell you that you have to ride them. They are packed so tight. You always lose a few. The job is to keep an airstream moving through the cages so they will not suffocate.

But the rest of what Joe Indian did was wrong. He was worse than trash. Men can get used to trash, but Joe bothered guys you would swear could not be bothered by anything in the world. Guys who had seen everything. Twenty years on the road, maybe. Twenty years of seeing people broken by stupidness. Crazy people, torn-up people, drunks. But Joe Indian even bothered guys who had seen all of that. One of the reasons might be that he never drank or did much. He never cared about anything. He just blew heavy black exhaust into load after load of white turkeys.

The rest of what he did was worse. He hated the load. Not the way any man might want to swear over some particular load. No. He hated every one of those turkeys on every load. Hated it personally the way one man might hate another man. He treated the load in a way that showed how much he despised the easy death that was coming to most of those turkeys—the quick needle thrust up the beak into the brain the way poultry is killed commercially. Fast. Painless. The night I saw him close was only a week before the trouble started.

He came into a stop in Harrodsburg. I was out of Tennessee loaded with a special order of upholstered furniture to way and gone up in Michigan and wondering how the factory had ever caught that order. The boss looked sad when I left. That made me feel better. If I had to fight tourists all the way up to the lake instead of my usual Cincinnati run, at least he had to stay behind and build sick furniture. When I came into the stop, I noticed a North Carolina job, one of those straight thirty or thirty-five footers with the attic. He was out of Hickory. Maybe one of the reasons I stopped was because there would be someone there who had about the same kind of trouble. He turned out to be a dark-haired and serious man, one who was very quiet. He had a load of couches on that were made to sell but never, never to use. We compared junk for a while, then looked through the window to see Joe Indian pull in with a truck that looked like a disease.

The Mack sounded bad, but from the appearance of the load it must have found seventy on the downgrades. The load looked terrible at close hand. Joe had cages that were homemade, built from siding of coal company houses when the mines closed down. They had horizontal slats instead of the vertical dowel rod. All you could say of them was that they were sturdy, because you can see the kind of trouble that sort of cage would cause. A bird would shift a little, get a wing-tip through the slat and the air stream would do the rest. The Mack came in with between seventy-five and a hundred broken wings fluttering along the sides of the crates. I figured that Joe must own the birds. No one was going to ship like that. When the rig stopped, the wings dropped like dead banners. It was hard to take.

"I know him," the driver who was sitting with me said.

"I know of him," I told the guy, "but nothing good."

"There isn't any, anymore," he said quietly and turned from the window. His face seemed tense. He shifted his chair so that he could see both the door and the restaurant counter. "My cousin," he told me.

I was surprised. The conversation kind of ran out of gas. We did not say anything because we seemed waiting for something. It did not happen.

All that happened was that Joe came in looking like his name.

"Is he really Indian?" I asked.

"Half," his cousin said. "The best half if there is any." Then he stopped talking and I watched Joe. He was dressed like anybody else and needed a haircut. His nose had been broken at one time. His knuckles were enlarged and beat-up. He was tall and rough looking, but there was nothing that you could pin down as unusual in a tough guy except that he wore a hunting knife sheathed and hung on his belt. The bottom of the sheath rode in his back pocket. The hilt was horn. The knife pushed away from his body when he sat at the counter.

He was quiet. The waitress must have known him from before. She just sat coffee in front of him and moved away. If Joe saw the driver beside me he gave no indication. Instead he sat rigid, tensed like a man being chased by something. He looked all set to hit, or yell, or kill if anyone had been stupid enough to slap him on the back and say hello. The restaurant was too quiet. I put a dime in the juke and pressed something just for the noise. Outside came the sound of another rig pulling in. Joe Indian finished his coffee, gulping it. Then he started out and stopped before us. He stared down at the guy beside me.

"Why?" the man said. Joe said nothing. "Because a man may come with thunder does not mean that he can ride the thunder," the driver told him. It made no sense. "A man is the thunder," Joe said. His voice sounded like the knife looked. He paused for a moment then went out. His rig did not pull away for nearly ten minutes. About the time it was in the roadway another driver came in angry and half-scared. He headed for the counter. We waved him over. He came, glad for some attention.

"Jesus," he said.

"An old trick," the guy beside me told him.

"What?" I asked.

"Who is he?" The driver was shaking his head.

"Not a truck driver. Just a guy who happens to own a truck."

"But how come he did that." The driver's voice sounded shaky.

"Did what?" I asked. They were talking around me.

The first guy, Joe's cousin, turned to me. "Didn't you ever see him trim a load?"

"What!"

"Truck's messy," the other driver said. "That's what he was saying. Messy. Messy." The man looked half-sick.

I looked at them still wanting explanation. His cousin told me. "Claims he likes neat cages. Takes that knife and goes around the truck cutting the wings he can reach . . . just enough. Never cuts them off, just enough so they rip off in the air stream."

"Those are live," I said.

"Uh huh."

It made me mad. "One of these days he'll find somebody with about thirty-eight calibers of questions."

"Be shooting around that knife," his cousin told me. "He probably throws better than you could handle a rifle."

"But why . . . ." It made no sense.

"A long story," his cousin said, "And I've got to be going." He stood up. "Raised in a coal camp," he told us. "That isn't his real name, but his mother was full Indian. His daddy shot coal. Good money. So when Joe was a kid he was raised Indian, trees, plants, animals, mountains, flowers, men . . . all brothers. His ma was religious. When he became 16 he was raised coal miner white. Figure it out." He turned to go.

"Drive careful," I told him, but he was already on his way. Before the summer was out Joe Indian was dead. But by then all of the truck traffic was gone from 150. The guys were routing through Lexington. I did not know at first because of trouble on the Michigan run. Wheel bearings in Sault Ste. Marie to help out the worn compressor in Grand Rapids. Furniture manufacturers run their lousy equipment to death. They expect every cube to run on bicycle maintenance. I damned the rig, but the woods up there were nice with stands of birch that jumped up white and luminous in the headlights. The lake and straits were good. Above Traverse City there were not as many tourists. But, enough. In the end I was pushing hard to get back. When I hit 150 it took me about twenty minutes to realize that I was the only truck on the road. There were cars. I learned later that the thing did not seem to work on cars. By then it had worked on me well enough that I could not have cared less.

Because I started hitting animals. Lots of animals. Possum, cat, rabbit, coon, skunk, mice, even birds and snakes . . . at night . . . with the moon tacked up there behind a thin and swirling cloud cover. The animals started marching, looking up off the road into my lights and running right under the wheels.

Not one of them thumped!

I rode into pack after pack and there was no thump, no crunch, no feeling of the soft body being pressed and torn under the drive axle. They marched from the shoulder into the lights, disappeared under the wheels and it was like running through smoke. At the roadside, even crowding the shoulder, larger eyes gleamed from nebulous shapes that moved slowly back. Not frightened; just like they were letting you through. And you knew that none of them were real. And you knew that your eyes told you they were there. It *was* like running through smoke, but the smoke was in dozens of familiar and now horrible forms. I tried not to look. It did not work. Then I tried looking hard. That worked too well, especially when I cut on the spot to cover the shoulder and saw forms that were not men and were not animals but seemed something of both. Alien. Alien. I was afraid to slow. Things flew at the windshields and bounced off without a splat. It lasted for ten miles. Ordinarily it takes about seventeen minutes to do those ten miles. I did it in eleven or twelve. It seemed like a year. The stop was closed in Harrodsburg. I found an all-night diner, played the juke, drank coffee, talked to a waitress who acted like I was trying to pick her up, which would have been a compliment . . . just anything to feel normal. When I went back to the truck I locked the doors and climbed into the sleeper. The truth is I was afraid to go back on that road.

So I tried to sleep instead and lay there seeing that road stretching out like an avenue to nowhere, flanked on each side by trees so that a man thought of a high speed tunnel. Then somewhere between dream and imagination I began to wonder if that road really did end at night. For me. For anybody. I could see in my mind how a man might drive that road and finally come into something like a tunnel, high beams rocketing along walls that first were smooth then changed like the pillared walls of a mine with timber shoring on the sides. But not in the middle. I could see a man driving down, down at sixty or seventy, driving deep towards the center of the earth and knowing that it was a mine. Knowing that there was a rock face at the end of the road but the man unable to get his foot off the pedal. And then the thoughts connected and I knew that Joe Indian was the trouble with the road, but I did not know why or how. I was shaking and cold. In the morning it was not so bad. The movement was still there but it was dimmed out in daylight. You caught it in flashes. I barely made Mount Vernon, where I connected with 25. The trouble stopped there. When I got home I told some lies and took a week off. My place is out beyond Lafollette, where you can live with a little air and woods around you. For a while I was nearly afraid to go into those woods.

When I returned to the road it was the Cincinnati run all over with an occasional turn to Indianapolis. I used the Lexington route and watched the other guys. They were all keeping quiet. The only people who were talking were the police who were trying to figure out the sudden shift in traffic. Everybody who had been the route figured if they talked about it, everyone else would think they were crazy. You would see a driver you knew and say hello. Then the two of you would sit and talk about the weather. When truckers stop talking about trucks and the road something is wrong.

I saw Joe once below Livingston on 25. His rig looked the same as always. He was driving full out like he was asking to be pulled over. You could run at speed on 150. Not on 25. Maybe he was asking for it, kind of hoping it would happen so that he would be pulled off the road for a while. Because a week after that and a month after the trouble started I heard on the grapevine that Joe was dead.

Killed, the word had it, by ramming over a bank on 150 into a stream. Half of his load had drowned. The other half suffocated. Cars had driven past the scene for two or three days, the drivers staring straight down the road like always. No one paid enough attention to see wheel marks that left the road and over the bank.

What else the story said was not good and maybe not true. I tried to dismiss it and kept running 25. The summer was dwindling away into fall, the oak and maple on those hills were beginning to change. I was up from Knoxville one night and saw the North Carolina job sitting in front of a stop. No schedule would have kept me from pulling over. I climbed down and went inside.

For a moment I did not see anyone I recognized, then I looked a second time and saw Joe's cousin. He was changed. He sat at a booth. Alone. He was slumped like an old man. When I walked up he looked at me with eyes that seemed to see past or through me. He motioned me to the other side of the booth. I saw that his hands were shaking.

"What?" I asked him, figuring that he was sick or had just had a close one.

"Do you remember that night?" he asked me. No lead up. Talking like a man who had only one thing on his mind. Like a man who could only talk about one thing.

"Yes," I told him, "and I've heard about Joe." I tried to lie. I could not really say that I was sorry.

"Came With Thunder," his cousin told me. "That was his other name, the one his mother had for him. He was born during an August storm."

I looked at the guy to see if he was kidding. Then I remembered that Joe was killed in August. It made me uneasy.

"I found him," Joe's cousin told me. "Took my car and went looking after he was three days overdue. Because . . . I knew he was driving that road . . . trying to prove something."

"What? Prove what?"

"Hard to say. I found him hidden half by water, half by trees and the brush that grows up around there. He might have stayed on into the winter if someone hadn't looked." The man's hands were shaking. I told him to wait, walked over and brought back two coffees. When I sat back down he continued.

"It's what I told you. But, it has to be more than that. I've been studying and studying. Something like this . . . always is." He paused and drank the coffee, holding the mug in both hands.

"When we were kids," the driver said, "we practically lived at each other's house. I liked his best. The place was a shack. Hell, my place was a shack. Miners made money then, but it was all scrip. They spent it for everything but what they needed." He paused, thoughtful. Now that he was telling the story he did not seem so nervous.

"Because of his mother," he continued. "She was Indian. Creek maybe, but west of Creek country. Or maybe from a northern tribe that drifted down. Not Cherokee because their clans haven't any turkeys for totems or names that I know of . . . ."

I was startled. I started to say something.

"Kids don't think to ask about stuff like that," he said. His voice was an apology as if he were wrong for not knowing the name of a tribe.

"Makes no difference anyway," he said. "She was Indian religious and she brought Joe up that way because his old man was either working or drinking. We all three spent a lot of time in the hills talking to the animals, talking to flowers . . . ."

"What?"

"They do that. Indians do. They think that life is round like a flower. They think animals are not just animals. They are brothers. Everything is separate like people."

I still could not believe that he was serious. He saw my look and seemed discouraged, like he had tried to get through to people before and had not had any luck.

"You don't understand," he said. "I mean that dogs are not people, they are dogs. But each dog is important because he has a dog personality the same as a man has a man personality."

"That makes sense," I told him. "I've owned dogs. Some silly. Some serious. Some good. Some bad."

"Yes," he said. "But, most important. When he dies a dog has a dog spirit the same way a man would have a man spirit. That's what Joe was brought up to believe."

"But they kill animals for food," I told him.

"That's true. It's one of the reasons for being an animal . . . or maybe, even a man. When you kill an animal you are supposed to apologize to the animal's spirit and explain you needed meat."

"Oh."

"You don't get it," he said. "I'm not sure I do either but there was a time . . . anyway, it's not such a bad way to think if you look at it close. But the point is Joe believed it all his life. When he got out on his own and saw the world he couldn't believe it anymore. You know? A guy acting like that. People cause a lot of trouble being stupid and mean."

"I know."

"But he couldn't quite not believe it either. He had been trained every day since he was born, and I do mean every day."

"Are they that religious?"

"More than any white man I ever knew. Because they live it instead of just believe it. You can see what could happen to a man?"

"Not quite."

"Sure you can. He couldn't live in the camp anymore because the camp was dead when the mines died through this whole region. He had to live outside so he had to change, but a part of him couldn't change, . . . then his mother died. Tuberculosis. She tried Indian remedies and died. But I think she would have anyway."

I could see what the guy was driving at.

"He was proving something," the man told me. "Started buying and hauling the birds. Living hand to mouth. But, I guess every time he tore one up it was just a little more hate working out of his system."

"A hell of a way to do it."

"That's the worst part. He turned his back on the whole thing, getting revenge. But always, down underneath, he was afraid."

"Why be afraid?" I checked the clock. Then I looked at the man. There was a fine tremble returning to his hands.

"Don't you see," he told me. "He still halfway believed. And if a man could take revenge, animals could take revenge. He was afraid of the animals helping their brothers." The guy was sweating. He looked at me and there was fear in his eyes. "They do, you know. I'm honest-to-God afraid that they do."

"Why?"

"When he checked out missing I called the seller, then called the process outfit where he sold. He was three days out on a one-day run. So I went looking and found him." He watched me. "The guys aren't driving that road."

"Neither am I," I told him. "For that matter, neither are you."

"It's all right now," he said. "There's nothing left on that road. Right outside of Harrodsburg, down that little grade and then take a hook left up the hill, and right after you top it . . . ."

"I've driven it."

"Then you begin to meet the start of the hill country. Down around the creek I found him. Fifty feet of truck laid over in the creek and not an ounce of metal showing to the road. Water washing through the cab. Load tipped but a lot of it still tied down. All dead of course."

"A mess."

"Poultry rots quick," was all he said.

"How did it happen?"

"Big animal," he told me. "Big like a cow or a bull or a bear . . . . There wasn't any animal around. You know what a front end looks like. Metal to metal doesn't make that kind of dent. Flesh."

"The stream washed it away."

"I doubt. It eddies further down. There hasn't been that much rain. But he hit something . . . ."

I was feeling funny. "Listen, I'll tell you the truth. On that road I hit everything. If a cow had shown up I'd have run through it, I guess. Afraid to stop. There wouldn't have been a bump."

"I know," he told me. "But Joe bumped. That's the truth. Hard enough to take him off the road. I've been scared. Wondering. Because what he could not believe I can't believe either. It does not make sense, it does not . . . ."

He looked at me. His hands were trembling hard.

"I waded to the cab," he said. "Waded out there. Careful of sinks. The smell of the load was terrible. Waded out to the cab hoping it was empty and knowing damned well that it wasn't. And I found him."

"How?"

"Sitting up in the cab sideways with the water swirling around about shoulder height and . . . . Listen, maybe you'd better not hear. Maybe you don't want to."

"I didn't wait this long not to hear," I told him.

"Sitting there with the bone handle of the knife tacked to his front where he had found his heart . . . or something, and put it in. Not in time though. Not in time."

"You mean he was hurt and afraid of drowning?"

"Not a mark on his body except for the knife. Not a break where, but his face . . . sitting there, leaning into that knife and hair all gone, chewed away. Face mostly gone, lips, ears, eyelids all gone. Chewed away, scratched away. I looked, and in the opening that had been his mouth something moved like disappearing down a hole . . . but, in the part of the cab that wasn't submerged there was a thousand footprints, maybe a thousand different animals . . . ."

His voice broke. I reached over and steadied him by the shoulder. "What was he stabbing?" the man asked. "I can't figure. Himself, or . . . ."

I went to get more coffee for us and tried to make up something that would help him out. One thing I agreed with that he had said. I agreed that I wished he had not told me.

The Troll

A troll lived in the cistern. She had known it for a long time, but (except once to her grandmother) she did not confide the knowledge. He was a green troll with three legs because he had lost one in an accident, but he was friendly. She did not believe any nonsense about trolls who ate billy goats.

When it was possible, as it sometimes was in that September of 1939 to slip out for a few moments after dark, she would hurry to the spring house and fetch a saucer of milk. She would place it by the pipe leading from the roof to the cistern. The milk was always gone in the morning. It proved her knowledge about the troll.

When the man came to clean the cistern the troll spent a very bad day huddling elongated in the pipe. He only escaped into the cool, bricked cistern with the setting of the sun. She hovered about the cistern all day, tapping gently on the pipe to reassure him with her presence, although occasionally her mother chased her away on errands.

"I'll be back," she would tell him. "I'll be back, I'll be back." Then she would go running, her bare feet over the still-warm earth to the mail box, to the neighbor's house, to the woodpile behind her own house where kindling for the cookstove was stacked.

The mountain behind the house remained green until late in

August. The small stream that had bounced, baltering about her feet and chilling them in the spring, became a trickle. The trickle still ran rapidly. To her the stream was acting with hurried care, the abandonment was gone. Later it became swollen with the autumn rains.

She knew where there was a huge fish who was trapped below an eddy. She did not confide that knowledge, either. On afternoons when the sun was hot against the persistent coolness of the forest, she ventured to the stream to speak gently to the fish who was very wild. Later, coming to know her, he would often hover in the prison of his pool, idly carried here, then there, by the jumping trickle of the stream. He always hid when she placed her hand in the water. She worried that the fish would be killed when the cold weather came.

"You worry too much," her mother often told her. "A pretty girl . . . a girl we expect things of . . . . You fritter away your time with a sick kitten. You needn't worry. The cat can take care of her kitten."

Her father always sided with her mother. He would look up from his work or reading. "Study hard this year. You did so well last year. Keep your good start going."

Her father always got the weekly paper. One night he laid it carefully beside him and said, "Damn." Then he said, "Goddamn."

"Hush. Don't swear." Her mother had been put out.

"This whole year. These past years. Depression. No work. And, now this coming. It *is* coming."

"I know."

To her the biggest difference in the year was in the way her parents acted.

It was the year in which her father spent most of the winter clearing the level acre of woodland left from her grandfather's farm. On Friday nights they did not visit the neighbors. On Saturdays they did not go in town. In the winter they made snow cream. One morning, when breakfast was late, her father's face looked funny. He rose from the table and walked to the barn, although no horses or cows lived there. There were not even any pigs, except in the next door neighbor's shed.

"Finish your breakfast," her mother said. Then her mother went to the barn.

That evening her parents took her to town for ice cream. They laughed, talking more to her than to each other. They did not seem quite the same. Her father bought a new picture puzzle. After it was put together they took it apart and traded to the neighbors for one they had not done.

"I got a fit. I got a fit!" she exclaimed each time she found a piece that matched. Once her father said, "So has the whole world."

She did not understand. Later, in the spring when there was talk of war she did not understand that either.

She went to fly a kite. Once she had owned an airplane but it had broken. It cost ten cents. She thought the kite much better. It only cost a nickle for the string. Her mother made it from lath, paste, and Christmas paper. It was red and white striped. The tail was made from an old yellow dress.

The kite field was by a grove not far from the school. The town road ran past the field. Often, people pulled off the road to talk and allow their children to play, or rested there before returning home from town. She did not think that it was Saturday. A great number of people would be there. She only thought it would be nice to show her grandmother the new kite.

There was no one at her grandmother's house when she banged the screen. She did not worry. Her grandmother would be next door up the road talking to a neighbor woman. While she waited she looked in the pantry and found a cookie. Then she found another.

Her grandmother returned and fussed about the cookies.

"As big as a house . . . ."

"See the kite," she said. "See the kite." Her grandmother went with her to the kite field to show her how they flew kites when she, her grandmother, was a little girl. People were always showing her how they did things when they were little.

And, they did not realize that she was no longer little. She was very grown up, taller than most children in her class, with brown hair nearly over her shoulders. She felt she could have flown the kite all alone. When they arrived at the kite field it was crowded. In the end she was glad her grandmother was with with her.

Remembering that spring, as she did once or twice in the year she was seven, she had the feeling but not the thought that perhaps she was not so grown up after all.

The kite went up, twitching and stuttering along its tight bow in the April breeze. It sailed high over the grove. She and her grandmother sat on a grassy bank by a parked car and a wagon to watch. She talked to her grandmother. Then she talked to the horse. There were several men leaning against the car. The kite tugged and dived. Her grandmother said she needed more string. She said she thought so, too.

"Grow grain," a voice said. They turned to look. The men walked toward them to stand by the wagon. The horse was very thin. "Grow grain." The speaker watched the children playing. "Nothing but grain. Grow corn. Grow wheat. Oats. Pile it up. Put it in. There's going to be a market."

"Like last time . . . ," another man spoke carefully.

"Not really. Folks were different then. Everybody excited and worked up. This time I'm just thinking that I'm putting in grain."

"There's talk of soybeans."

"Well, yes. There's talk. But the Sages' boy. You know him. Went to school at the capitol. He says grow grain."

"War?"

"Bound to be."

"What is war?" she asked. "War!" the little boys yelled and ran around the kite field and through the trees of the grove.

"Jobs," a man said. "God forgive me. I haven't worked and haven't worked . . . ."

"David and Goliath," her grandmother told her. "That was a war."

"Are we David or Goliath?"

Her grandmother seemed troubled and showed it in her face. "I don't know," she said.

Her grandmother's voice passed the trouble on. It made her a little afraid. Suddenly she was defiant. "We have a troll," she said. "He lives in the cistern."

"A troll?"

"Yes. And the cat has five kittens and one of them is yellow and black."

Her grandmother understood. "I lived in that house when I was a little girl. That was one of the first houses around here. The troll lived there then."

One of the men chuckled. "Maybe he's the one that gets out every twenty years." The other men laughed.

"Wind up your kite," her grandmother told her. "This is not good talk for you to hear."

They returned home to mend a tiny rip in the kite with paper and paste. A few weeks later school let out. She had passed to the second grade.

"Read this summer," her mother told her. "The most important of all is reading." On Wednesdays, before the heat settled in to bounce summer off the slate roof of the house, her mother would take her down the road and in town to the library. She was allowed to pick one book she wanted to read and one her mother wanted her to read. The ones her mother picked were always too hard.

"What is this word?"

"Pro-tect. Protect. You could have figured it out. By sound. It means that the mother rabbit is keeping the little rabbit from being hurt."

"Read it to me."

"I like to read to you. I wish I could. You must read to yourself and learn."

The summer hurried. It opened full in June. The dirt in the garden was black against the green plants. The flowers on the plants were yellow and white. Sometimes a hen from up the road squeezed clucking under the front gate and had to be shooed home. Once a pig got in, grunting and rooting up a row of radishes. She helped her father and mother in the garden, weeding and turning the black earth around corn, beans, tomatoes. One day in the garden her father spoke to her mother. He was very serious.

"I must go and try. Things are opening up a little. In the city."

Her mother seemed sad. "I suppose so. We have to do something."

The next day her father left for the city. It was lonely without him. He did not come home on the Fourth of July. He came home later, nearly a week later. He brought fireworks. That night he sent skyrockets walking up the summer wind while pinwheels fizzed and sparkled from nails on the barn.

"A job. I have a job."

"Will it last? Oh, I'm so glad. Will it last?"

"In the city. Yes, it will last. It's not the best kind of job but it is a job."

She sometimes listened to her parents talk before she went to sleep. That night, after her father came home, she was drowsy from the exciting day. Words came to her, undisturbing through the warmth of approaching sleep.

"Will we have to move?"

"No. It isn't that good a job. I hope for something better."

"But you will be away."

"Yes. It isn't far. Twenty-five miles, but, without a car. I think to come home one evening a week and after work on Saturdays. That will give us Sundays."

"She will miss you as much as I will." Had she been fully awake she would have known that her mother nodded to her room.

"She is growing up," her father said. "She cannot stay small forever. I wish she could. This is a part of her growing up."

"There was a piece in the paper. A piece that told how they get frightened with all the talk going on. A doctor wrote it."

"There are doctors to tell us everything except what we need. Will the doctor be her teacher, her friend? Will he keep her from talk among the relatives . . . . No," her father said. "The hell with the doctor. But, we will do the best we can."

"I wish you wouldn't swear."

"I wish there wasn't going to be a war. Why wouldn't a man swear?"

She came awake. The word brought her back. She crept to the door to look into the living room which centered around the cold iron of the stove that had been dull red and hot during the winter. Her father was in an old rocker before the front window. He looked unhappy. Her mother was sitting quietly in another chair. They were very still. She knew they had heard her get up.

"Do they hurt children?" she asked. "David and Goliath. Did they hurt children?"

Her mother seemed about to cry. Her father stood up slowly and walked to her. He picked her up and carried her to the rocker. He held her.

"There is something bad going on in the world," he said. "But that badness stops at our front fence. Don't worry." She found that being held was better than ever. She was more sleepy than she thought.

After that, Wednesday was book day and father day. On Thursday mornings he was gone again. She saw him very little. On the weekends she would show how well her reading had progressed. She worked hard to miss no words.

On weekdays when her reading was done she helped her mother in the garden. She ran errands. She sat watching as her mother and grandmother canned tomatoes or made jelly. The kitchen on those days was hot with huge kettles sitting on the stove.

"I wish your daddy was here to help," her grandmother said.

"Underfoot," her mother said, and smiled. "I wish he were here too."

"You were lucky," her grandmother said to her mother.

"Yes. He is a good man." Her mother smiled a different kind of smile. "He does not like the job . . . ."

"But, he does it."

"Yes, and doesn't complain. We miss him. I wish he were home more. The place is getting behind. The cistern, a gate hinge broken, the big door of the barn . . . ."

"You can hire a little bit of help now."

"I may have to. When he's home there isn't time."

Sometimes she was allowed to go to the house beyond her grandmother's to play with friends who lived there. At other times she played in the woods at the base of the mountain. Once or twice she climbed higher, exploring. It was late in August when she found the fish.

"You should meet my other friend," she told the fish on her second visit. "He is like you. He stays in one place. I will tell him to visit you." She ran home to explain to the troll about her friend. The third time she visited the fish he seemed a bit more tame. She thought the troll had come and it made her glad.

School started immediately after Labor Day. Her teacher was younger than her first grade teacher had been. She was very pretty. When she spoke her voice was sometimes like laughing. At other times it was not like crying but seemed stretched or distant. Her first teacher had been the same all the time. With this teacher she learned to listen each morning to the voice so she would know what the teacher would do.

"Reports," her teacher said. "It is something new we will try this year. I want each of you to tell about something you like."

"It sounds nice," her mother said when she heard. "What will you tell about?"

She did not know. There were a great many things. She kept a cigar box in the attic. In it was a plaster dog and some other things. Her Sunday School pin for one. She thought she might tell about the box.

"The report is tomorrow. And the day after . . . ."

Her mother interrupted. "I'm sorry. I think he won't be home until Saturday. There is a school for him at night. He will be a foreman." She pulled a note from beneath a dish on the table. "But, he will be home Saturday. We'll have a fine time." She smiled. "You'll have a whole week to tell him about."

That night it rained. She was sitting on the front porch and heard the rain moving through a cut in the mountains toward the house. A cool wind was ahead of the rain, kicking the tree branches. A shower of leaves fluttered through the night. Her mother was inside. She could hear her moving about. Her mother was singing softly. She did not feel like singing.

During the summer she had sometimes been allowed to play in the rain. Now she jumped from the porch to get a little bit wet. When the rain arrived it was hard and cold. She was soaking almost immediately and caught a chill. Her mother sent her to bed.

The water from the cistern had always been cold. She knew it but had never been bothered. As she lay in her bed trying to get warm she listened to the hard rain against the window. There was the sound of water running down the pipe into the cistern. Without knowing why she knew that the troll was gone. Later, she understood that the reason was the cold.

It was still raining in the morning. She wore her boots and carried her mother's umbrella. As she left she hesitated by the cistern. Then she went on with only a glance. It was deserted.

In the middle of the morning they had reports. The teacher called her name. She stood up.

"I have a friend who is a fish." A boy laughed. She turned on him. "He is nicer than you." The teacher made everyone be quiet while she told about the fish. She wanted to make a picture. How the fish lay in the jumping pool, surrounded by green weeds and the shining pebbles that came tumbling down the mountain. She wanted to show them how he looked, golden and speckled against the shadowy black rock lying at the bottom of the pool. How sometimes he swam under a ledge of the rock to sleep.

When she was done the teacher said that it was a lovely report. She asked the class if there were any questions. The boy raised his hand.

"That fish is a trout. They are good to eat. If I found him I'd eat him." He looked at her. "I'm going to find him after school," he said.

She knew he was a mean boy. She knew he would do what he said, and began to cry. At noon she was very nervous. The teacher sent her home.

"He'll not do it," her mother said. They sat in the kitchen for a long while talking. "He will not do it . . . ." It was the first time she had ever seen her mother terribly angry.

Her mother took her to her grandmother's house, then went in town. That evening her father came home. It was only Tuesday. He seemed angry. "The creek may be up. It may have risen enough in the night for the fish to get away. A fish . . . . "

"Please," her mother said, "this is important."

"A lot of things are important. I'm sorry. Yes, I suppose it is."

Her father fetched a large net and a bucket. The three of them went through the late dusk, following the creek to the pool where the fish was trapped. The fish was still there. He was very angry and flopped in the net. Her father carried him downstream to release him in deep water. She was very worried and tried to see, but only heard the fish drop into the black water with barely a splash. Then they went in town and had an ice cream.

The ice cream tasted nearly as good as usual. Her father said that he must return to the city. They walked with him to the bus station. While they walked and while they waited for the bus her father was very serious. Her mother seemed worried. Her father spoke to her in a careful, grown-up way which she was able to understand.

"You are a good, big girl," he said. He hugged her, kissed her mother and got on the bus. She and her mother walked home. On the way they did not say very much. When they arrived home it was the same as always except that the troll was still gone and sounds from the darkness told them that the neighbor's sow was plundering the remnants of the garden.

Thermopylae

Well before dawn, when the sky was sparked with stars that washed in a great band of marble brilliance above the hills, he left the small house and walked through the close-built streets picking up the goats and a few sheep. The work was simple and he had been doing it all his life. It had seen him become old with knowledges that were more than he could explain.

By the time dawn was fading the stars, he had the flock out of the village and on the lower reaches of the hills. At sunrise they would be grazing the scrub, fat-bellied, lean-backed, their hooves sure among the tumble of rock over which he had to move slowly, depending more each year on the unpredictable dog. He liked the goats. Although they were more trouble than the sheep, he had never really liked the sheep.

This morning there was difference, although it was felt and not to be thought about. Each house was still. Many had fled and all were quiet. The rustle of the chickens as he approached seemed louder because of the stillness, and the early voice of Sodamos' detestable rooster lived in the air like the swing and clang of axes. He shuddered with the unthinking required for this different morning and felt offended. There was no movement in the houses. He untethered three goats, was turning, confronted the ruffian Sodamos who was the father of a dead man. There was no sleep about Sodamos' form. He did not rub his hair or eyes in the darkness. His beard was against his chest and pointed nowhere.

"You go to work anyway," Sodamos said. "You are crazy, I know it."

"It is morning," the old man said about the rooster. It was a morning of hammers.

"You call this morning? This is not morning." Sodamos was also old. Since yesterday. He disappeared limping around the side of the house. There was a quick sound, the catch, squawk, the flutter, a neck being wrung. As the old man took the goats down the street, the indifferent dog padding ahead of their hooves, the morning was vibrating with the distinct thump of the rooster body as it pumped blood into the darkness.

"So it will be with you, stupid." He spoke softly to the dog over the backs of the flock. He did not want to break the silence. Nothing great had yet happened to the dog.

On the night before, when the light had faded from pink to blue to purple, with blackness in the cuts between the hills, the news had arrived. The great pass of Thermopylae was taken and the lost defenders were said to be symbols. Greece would flame with the spirit of resistance. It was also said that the defense had been outnumbered like a single fish in a net.

So it was said. News leaped fast in these hills, and where news leaped Persian armies would follow. In the dark morning the gravity of the news was contained in more than silence. It was in the judgmental spaces between sounds and movements. It did not matter that some spoke softly with fatal heroism or tragic pride. Fools sought consolation in such lies.

He had been at his house after returning the last of the goats. His knowledge was in the sound, and that had been the feel of rapid movement toward the center of the village, the murmur that seemed to turn corners of packed and breathless streets; a murmur that was wide and anguished and terrible because it was low and constant. Then a woman screamed, and the scream rose in the evening, rising and rising, walking ranges of sky and hills like an agony released from rock. Then the scream choked. The murmur stopped. There was this silence.

"Our men who went to war beside the Spartans are dead."

"Are the Spartans dead?"

"The Spartans are also dead, but our men who went to war beside them are dead."

The dog circled, circled back, circled again, and the bunching flock settled to stream through a narrow breach between rocks from which they would leave the lower road of the village and spread onto the first reaches of the hill.

"Why do you wait until now to do well," he asked the dog. It was a big, gray dog, heavy shanked and heavy furred, but very young. Sometimes it was silly.

The problem he was wondering at was not even one of survival, but one of continuance. It seemed that an old man should know something of that.

Rocks split sometimes in the sun; shattering, shaping, crossing forms over years beyond him. As he passed through the narrow cut it was possible to understand that once perhaps all had been a single rock.

Sheep were occasionally known to graze on the wool but not the flesh of dead sheep. One did not know what to make of such great knowledges. The old man brushed flakes from a cool rock that rose from the ground like a squat monument. Later the rock would be hot and throw no shadow.

It was a time of death. Separated men of separated cities and towns and even villages would be harvested by separated men of Persia; blood upon rock faces and the stones of streets, screams of women and the whining fear of patriarchal lard-vats with down-dropping eyes and hair. Fat-bellied, skinny-rumped, like the bobbing, bag-juggling of the driven flock. His worthless dog would snarl at death but the goats would not. Sheep cried in terror when killed for the spit.

Following the flock he felt the heat of breath in his mouth and thought about the evening wine and talk; about the spread legs and wet, open mouths of women. It was something he understood about the work and he had not thought of such things in years. These were kill thoughts. They ground the loins of old men and drove young men mad. Perhaps today they could be afforded.

Because there would not have been many years of the wine and talk and work left, anyway. It seemed unclean, this sudden world that denied old lives and spit out Persians.

The goats worked up the hill and when the sun rose it came laying an orange glow across their backs. Then the sun moved higher and the whiteness came. It was always like that, whiteness in the scrub and across the red rock. Turning, one could see the village like powdered rock that had been pushed into square shapes to endure the wind. It was an old man's illusion, but he had seen powdered rock in many ways and places.

Persians did not care who they killed.

"They eat roasted dog," he called to his dog. The dog was a long way off, far up the hill and to the left. It sat on its haunches panting, waiting, by its presence forcing the flock right. The old man moved left and up. There was dismay among the goats because this was not customary. On other days he arranged to move high only by noon. The flock was hurried forward and two goats broke and ran. The dog moved well, seriously running and rounding them in.

He knew what he was doing while he was doing it and realized that this was what he had intended from the first. Above was a narrow opening that constituted a cleft in the rock big enough to conceal a man. His father had slept away the noons in that cleft, shaded from the rock-splitting sun while his dog worked. Later, when his father was old, the job and the cleft became his. These were kill thoughts again. It would be wrong to sit in that place and think of one's father.

He turned to glance back over the village before stooping to enter the cleft. Alpenoi would fall first. Probably they were taking the heat at Alpenoi right now, and tomorrow or late today the villages would be swept. The flock would be used for food, the people for various reasons. Finally, it was obvious that the only continuance was for a man to preserve himself. This concealment was unknown, even in the village. It was necessary to stoop, turn and back into the small cleft.

The sides were smooth from the shoulders of shepherds and it was his custom during the noons to sit first between the stones, in the powder of rubbed rock, and move his shoulders against the sides. It was a gratification and a customary preparation for sleep. Behind him the cleft widened but it was very low. Dark. Cool. Large enough for a man to lie down, but one crawled in. There was no room to sit.

Again the mind knew more than could be explained and he admired the plan his mind had discovered. In taking the flock at the proper time he had made his day seem usual to others. On this day he would return the flock early, then circle the village and return to the cleft to wait out the rapid desolation. In two days there would be no Persians. They would not stay in a broken village.

The sun was blooming like a pit of fire, flooding the hill and pinioning the flock which would soon be driven to the overhang and small shade. Across the white and brown and red of the slope, heat rose in waves as palpable as steaming springs. The rubbing of his shoulders caused him to feel tranquil and ready to turn to sleep. Once, when visiting the sea, he had met a sailor who said that there was a place where men were black and trees grew thirty times a man's height. The sailor had been drunk.

Sleep was a continuing pleasure, one did not need the hot legs of women. Nearby he heard the movement of some of the goats, and when he slept his mind seemed puzzled, his dreams like arrows of impulse that shadowed the brightness of his new knowledge. He would be preserved. It was while he was sleeping that Sodamos found him.

The dog was barking and the old man woke and was startled until he saw Sodamos' feet and knew that they belonged to a villager. A shadow covered the front of the cleft and he could not sit up. Outside the dog barked and yapped, bouncing about the legs to cause a second shadow that moved very black in the sun. The useless dog had not barked in time. The dog had betrayed him.

"Come out, it is necessary." Sodamos' voice was low. The growl of the voice silenced the dog.

"What has happened?" He recognized the voice. He did not want to hear that voice. Sodamos was capable.

"Come out."

"I have a knife."

"So have I." The voice seemed almost pleased. "I also have a club. I can break your feet or cut them off."

"Stand back, I am no match for you."

"Not even by stealth." The legs moved back and the old man wriggled forward, attained a sitting position, and sat blinking his eyes as he became accustomed to the light. Sodamos waited.

"What do you want?" His mind was in a great hurry. This Sodamos was not of the hill. The hill was the prerogative of shepherds.

"I bring Iannos." Sodamos stepped further away as the old man's eyes became accustomed to the light.

Sodamos' grandson was held by its mother. A detestable, squalling brat, but silent now, and the mother was a small and quiet woman. There would be no justice here.

"They will starve." He rose to his feet.

"No," Sodamos said, "but they will be very hungry. We cannot even tether a goat which would be seen." He threw a water bag into the cleft.

"Are they so close?"

"Before evening, surely. Tonight we will drink wine elsewhere."

He would be lost. His mind tumbled. "I can betray you," he told Sodamos. "I can refuse to gather the flock."

Sodamos touched his knife. "You die quickly and all at once with an ax, not in little pieces." His voice was calm but his face was rough, the eyes deep beneath the forehead and determined. His beard now had direction. "You are crazy, I know that, but you are still a man."

"Ianus should care for his son."

"Ianus is dead. He followed Thespians who followed Spartans. To play those games is to be a fish trying to fly."

"Why did he go?" He wondered at himself, trying to gain time on a lost hill.

"He was religious. Gather the flock."

At first he moved slowly, but the dog behaved well and although the goats did not know or trust Sodamos the man was some help. By the time the sun was casting their brief shadows eastward they had the flock gathered and pointed home. Sodamos looked back to check the concealment and it was good. The old man despaired. Nowhere in the hills was there a place as good. There were other places but they were obvious.

"You should have taken them to a walled town."

"You are crazier than usual. Walls are like piled dung. The people of the towns are already dead."

"You know this?"

"Would you leave a village to hide in a town?"

Always the descent was too fast, the goats homeward to water, and the dog bounding and yappy, playing the fool as it attended to duty. The dog had betrayed him and was useless. In despair he tried to hate the dog. The flock bunched and rubbed, jiggled and bumped and cried. They milled before the narrow breach in the rock as the dog herded them through and onto the road. Sodamos stopped him.

"I will wait here."

"Why?" As he asked he saw why.

"Others from the village will come. The place is not known, but someone will remember that you have a place."

"There are plenty of ways to enter onto the hill."

"This is the customary way. They will come here. A man can put a stopper in this place."

"You would kill your friends?"

"Now they are my enemies." Sodamos' voice was again a growl. His capable hands raised the club to his chest, wrists thick, shoulders no longer old. He stood in the narrow cut of rock with spread legs and there was not much room on either side. "I am not sorry," he said.

The old man turned and walked as rapidly as possible after the flock. It was only a short distance to the village, and the dog was already leading. The flock bunched along the familiar road, jostling, fast-stepping. Old legs were not trustworthy. He followed them quickly and dropped them off quickly, tethering some beside deserted houses.

It would be possible to move wide of the village, enter again onto the hill and perhaps overcome the woman. In the streets there was little movement, but now there was sound in the houses. Dust was soft and small rocks rolled beneath his feet. When he arrived at the house he used a tether to secure the dog. The dog had never been tied before. It whined and struggled, lapped the water he gave it, and howled as he left.

East and toward the Persians one might circle the village unseen. West was Sodamos who was not sorry, and it seemed to him that those words were an explanation that his mind did not yet know. Soon there would be fury between those rocks. He touched his knife and felt more than heard the rapid talk in the houses. It would be possible to tie the knife firmly to a staff to make a thrusting-spear. He turned west. It was also possible that Sodamos could not hold that breach alone.

With No Breeze

Hurd was our friend in younger days when we were lean with the upper airs in our lungs. Pike and I breathe even taller air now, but it is recirculated. A well-combed variety that contains neither smoke nor living perfume.

Transitory days. Our learning was well impressed by fogs, winds, and the distant glitter of the Charles seen interruptedly from the whispering crown of an oak. Young visions. They were thrilling, crackling with the scent, slap and flutter of leaves. "Days of the Indignant Robin," according to Pike who is singer and epigramist and extoller of love.

He climbed with us, Pike. And he is still sometimes able to drop his practiced negro smile for a quite natural one, so that his dark and familiar face seems no longer removed to the enigmatic solitude of five million record album jackets.

Transitory days. Myself, a self-styled Paul now only slightly amazed by his Saul, but bitter because he no longer bitterly struggles. Author of timely work. Respectable beyond the vulgarity of blue Sunday suits. Myself, remembering the climbing, remembering the sometime gleaming sunshades of yellow and green that remain as real as the rock-mixed earth of Massachusetts where we sweated and sang with a young pride in our work-hardened muscles.

We came to San Francisco. Hurd remained to plant. Now a letter says that he is dead. Dispatched by the nearly casual reference of a friend who wrote with the human perversity that delights in inflicting first pain that he "believed" I already knew. I will write thanks to my friend.

I called Pike about the letter. His secretary appointed me to lunch after a respectable two-day wait. I kept the appointment. But, before our meeting and since, I have considered Hurd and the something ungainly that creates feathers when there is no breeze to float them. I have also considered memory where voices whisper that the textures of intonation are the most palpable remains of the past.

"In California, they say, trees grow to three hundred feet and the lightning plays in the tops to scatter a ton of wood in the explosion."

"So! To see. I would like . . . ."

"And yet, the trees do not die."

"Deep. The root."

Then a black hand caressing the throat of a guitar and a lyrically instinctive comment, now long past sung into the air and unremembered by the singer.

> The tap drives deep, it questions down,
> Underfooting in the ground,
> Stir the rock the centuries round,
> The answer come up green.

"Good! Good!" At such times Hurd did not seem so old and thick of body.

"Not good," Pike would grin, very pleased although one understood that his pleasure was not with himself.

Thus the ear remembers after fatigue is forgotten.

We were expatriots. Hurd of country. Pike and myself of land. We worked at planting, climbing and pruning in Cambridge where the trees of the University have carefully ordered branches. According to our touch. Our touch.

Hurd came from Germany, Pike from Illinois, and I from North

Carolina where the spring is a crash of rhododendron that stands leggy and tall in the forests surrounding the mountain roads.

The sums now seem so simple. Pike. Tall. Black. Loving. Coming from the fields of rich Illinois farmland to sing because he believed he could be a good man who taught with music. It is a quick tale. There is too much compassion, the resonance of love extolling over unsubdued strings the fact of men and trees and grasses. The depth is too passionate. His admirers have hailed him as a sort of chocolate-covered Thoreau, although none see deeply enough to know that in such terms Thoreau was an Americanized Jesus. Pike is revered by a generation that is emotionally but not thoughtfully stylistic. A generation that has made him rich and missed his point exactly. He wanted to tell them to love one another, content that the idea was not new but only exciting. He is very wealthy.

The sums. I came to write. It seems that what I wanted to write was, "I am a gentle man, part white but mostly Indian, who will explain away secular worlds." It seems that I was going to tell of the importance of being compassionately a man and doing reverence to life. Religious-like, I was going to say, "I love you," which was not the message of Pike who had one greater than his ego.

It did not work out. At least, it has not worked out. I stand tall in the wrong places, am too well thought of for long usage.

Hurd came to live. Perhaps he came hoping to express his life. If so, he was courageous. The death of his expression had been in process, in slow movement beneath ancestral shadow, for over forty years. If he came with a hope it causes a wound I do not like to consider, that I am scarcely brave enough to entertain. That a man like Hurd . . . . Well, in Salt Lake City there is a statue portraying an emigrant Mormon family, the woman bearing a child, the man pulling in the shafts of a cart their heaped belongings, a child walking . . . the family walking across a desert under a certain sun and surrounded only by horizon. A tell-tale of the human spirit that causes in me an ecstasy of honor and grief. . . . so Hurd may have hoped.

Having known him in age I can see him in youth, the tale beginning in the writer imagination. I know how he would have been, standing proud but half-shy in the full strength of the young during that enormous time when men's hearts burned and their souls were filled with smoke and swastikas.

Hurd would have been studying a leaf or watching a bird as familiar to him as sunlight as it fell with a flicker of feather into the high top of an oak. In my imagination I see him standing. Young. Filled with a country innocence. Standing. He would watch people pass as they babbled the familiar confusion of a familiar language. Then, escaping in shyness, he would grasp bark, and with an upward heave disappear into branches with a man gracefulness that need not apologize to the bird.

Because Hurd would have been an ornament on his landscape as pine boughs are used to decorate mantles at Christmas or hollyhocks are grown near country doorways. An ornament of youth. In his age he was changed. Discipline locked him as root fungus does a tree, throwing its choking spine up one side at a time so that the plant lives several years into its certain death.

But I know these things intuitively. Both Pike and I were prejudiced and displeased when we first met him.

We had wintered off Harvard Square on savings from summer jobs. We worked well that winter, were frugal and content, although the warmth of the old apartment house was mostly illusory. In late March we faced the perpetual reality. The rent was coming down. To pay for that, with or without heat, we took jobs.

"What can you do?" Pike asked. He lay on a bed, so tall that his feet hung over the end. His canvas shoes were ratty, his hair needed cutting and he was down to his last laundered shirt. I mentally surveyed my own appearance, bulky but unfat, jeans and a sweat shirt, flat forehead and un-Roman nose. I admitted with caution that I could do nearly anything necessary.

Pike studied a paper, shaking his head as he checked off all of the things he was not: accountant, adjuster, advertising space man, banking apprentice, ball bearing fitter, carpenter . . . . "Can you climb?" he asked.

"Mountains?"

"Trees, man."

We agreed that we had both climbed trees at about age ten. Our clothing was too light for a New England spring but we could move quickly. Our pockets were also light. On the walk to the employer's office we looked at trees. We were impressed by their immensity. At first we were cowed and felt foolhardy. Then our youth and inexperience allowed a bravado, a resolute gaiety.

We signed affidavits, took medicals and were told that we were insured. The employer was an older man who walked with a limp. One shoulder rode higher than the other. An inauspicious beginning. It was certain that he knew we had overstated our experience. Without emphasis, yet the warning was present, he reached behind him to rub the high-riding shoulder and told us not to step back to admire our work. Sobering. In the next few days we met other men who worked for the company. Many of them were summer help and inexpert. Men were occasionally known to refuse a tree. In our minds this seemed an onus, whether based on a sensible estimate of danger or on fear. We decided that we would never refuse a tree and we never did. But from the first we were assigned to Hurd. The decisive advantage.

He was a strange discovery, our foreman. A stooped figure standing in the gloom of the old barn that served as a company garage. A curious teacher, as one with and resembling our oldest of the company trucks; the both smelling of loam, tree-cuttings, chemical fertilizer, new rope, pine rakings, and pitch. A small man. Hurd could not have weighed very much. Compact with heavy limbs, he was designed in squares. Thick. Soil does things to a man. He limped from kneeling too often in wet earth. His hands were gnarled with the lifetime of soil cracks that seal over sore joints. Hurd was too big to be a gnome and yet he seemed disproportionate to a man. His work clothing fitted. He was of some store-bought size. His heavy accent carried speech so direct that it could only come from a minimal knowledge of the language.

A strange discovery. Pike and I spoke of it during the evening as we felt our stretched muscles. Unlike Pike, I had not known prejudice as hatred but as sport, which leads to the same self-negation and doubt. While every Negro is no longer Sambo, the Indian is still Cochise, or perhaps even Rain-In-The-Face. Which is to say that one is not taken very seriously, not even as threat. A strange discovery, because in Hurd's thick speech there had been reason for us to find that attitude. We did not like ourselves.

"German." Pike picked up his guitar and it spoke softly, the sound seeking direction.

"We lived in Newport News during forty-two and forty-three."

"But German. Should we ask? Men believe what they deny."

"I was a kid. Gardener. Party member? A man could become a gardener."

In the following weeks we did better as our understanding of the work increased. Our understanding of Hurd came slowly. It started first with the climbing.

We were frightened and ashamed of our fear. The confidence of our youth was shaken. We could hardly have conceived ourselves dead, yet there was a hint of mortality in our sore bodies and in each involuntary gasp that came when we had nearly committed to an inexperienced hand-hold.

We had to learn trust. We high-climbed nearly from the beginning. A cut limb jumping on the ground man's line, moving his braced feet in jerks, is a deadly and capricious weight. It makes an arc near you while you are tied in and braced, clutching a chainsaw that you are too off-balanced to lower. All of this happens at killing distance from the ground, often near high voltage lines.

We learned to work with care, to trust no part to speed or impetuosity. Had we been with a lesser man we might have been injured or fired. Hurd pointed the way. He climbed with one of us, then with the other. He spoke little during the first days, only listening to our talk and Pike's singing. We took his reserve to mean criticism and were resentful.

A tree does not defy you. It exists; bark, leaders, leaves, all of a piece. It speaks a permanence that creates a profound impression on your mind. The tangibility is absolute. You are subdued in attempting to match something so actual. Not all of them are so. Some of the maples, some of the sycamores, nearly all of the lindens are like ladders, which is the way you think. We did well with rope climbing on poplar. We enjoyed a spate of small willows, cherries, and a half dozen Washington Hawthornes. (I love to work hawthornes. Carefully. They command respect.) But, on the fourth day of work, in fog, and after heavy fog on the preceding night, we broke out high gear and faced an English Elm.

I remember: a one hundred foot, single leader tree disappearing high into the fog, its first main branching at forty-five or fifty feet. In my memory it recalls a reality bulking huge against later experience that holds too much of dream, too much of pretense.

I approached the tree with little more knowledge than of how to begin. The harness, old style and Hurd's preference, seemed clumsy after having used a saddle. The tree took an amazing amount of line. Ascending, the spurs felt made of tin, their bite too soft, although the ankle pains returned and were familiar. The pressure of the harness was uneven. It was rigged too loose. My tool rope was a weight, like a dead tail coiled, and I suddenly felt like an animal dying by inches. On elms there is an occasional looseness about the spurs although the bark just passed was sound. I dared not look down and thought of the law of acceleration of falling bodies.

Slowly. The first lateral was shrouded in fog. The bark was not wet. Yet, the fog seemed in the bark. Slick. And the first lateral was high. At fifteen feet I thought myself much higher, which is common, and found a fear that tasted woody and sour. It quelled my senses. I pushed it back with wonder. It seemed to have nothing to do with me, face to bark with an elm. I tried to overcome fear by not thinking of it and wished to press my forehead to the tree's roughness.

Beneath me Hurd was preparing to climb. I could not believe that I was there. Forced to be first up an elm. I complained to myself between gritted teeth. He was experienced and could have rigged a line. At twenty-five feet I heard his spurs and heavy breathing. Then he waited. I went on. My hands were cold and unlimber.

There was a gust of wind moving in the fog which tokened the far off tide change. It was not strong but it moved my hair and caused the first lateral to creak. I froze. From the ground came the sound of too much movement. Pike was also afraid and keeping busy.

I tried to break a spur to climb and could not. I'll descend then, I thought, and could not break for that. I could not will movement, wished to be courageous, but had no conscious control. There was another gust of wind. I pulled up hard to the tree which increased the fear because it decreased the backward leaning leverage. My hands were throbbing and losing strength. There was a tremble in my knees.

"Song, ground man. Something funny you sing, yah?" Hurd's voice seemed to be asking only for entertainment. He was just below me. I felt his hand on my foot, not pressing it upward but massaging the ankle, his strong fingers causing a countering hurt through the heavy boot.

From the ground came the slap of a rope's end against the bed of the truck. Pike joined his rhythm slowly, changing suddenly from the smack of the rope to a metered clapping of his hands. He sang a new tune and lyric, his improvisation, his song for climbing trees.

I was suddenly embarrassed. My hands felt better. I gained the first lateral to the measures of the song and looked down. It was an incredible distance through the fog. I saw them both. Hurd's face, small, round-nosed, un-beautiful. It was not far away. Pike, leaning backward; young, smooth-textured, clapping and singing into the tree. Their force was beyond desperate situations; the love of men for men. I felt very important to them and tried to mask my embarrassment.

A few early people were attracted by the singing. I stood on the lateral watching and thought that Hurd should not be fifty feet up a tree. He looked so used. He passed me, braced and threw a line to a secondary leader.

"A first time for all there must be." He spoke confidentially as if there were some third party to hear. "To do this now. Is nothing." The trouble was over. I never really feared a tree again although I have not climbed Eucalyptus or Sequoia. Men do climb them.

And so Hurd had been kind or perhaps only commanding in an emergency he had probably seen before. We spoke of it that night. Talking. We talked incessantly in those days. Studying without knowing we were studying.

"I was afraid. Hurd was different today."

"Perhaps he's shy." Pike rubbed his ankles. "Whatever, he pulled us through a very bad one."

Us. That is like Pike. That is his kind of commitment.

"Are you hungry?" I asked. "Payday is day after. We can hock the typewriter and eat until closing."

"Agreed. You're in no shape for work.

We ate and did not worry about novels or trees or aches. We sang, Pike in that throbbing voice that so plainly understands the error that is human pain; I, subdued of voice and admiring. We sang with relief and because the night was mild, like one gift of the beginning spring.

The spring. The work. As both progressed we became more excited, reacting with a vigor that was unique in our experience. We rollicked like students in a courtly musical, singing, welcoming old people who scuffed by, crones blinking in the new sun after their cold and rabbit-warren winter. Our spring was rare. Neither Pike nor I had a woman. No part of us was in love except as we were always in love. Still, the spring held a warm and transcendent mystery. There was a woman softness to our moods. We felt the gentle tenseness that comes from beauty, perhaps not unmixed with the tensions of sexual desire. Yet, the site is in the temples. A prayerful man, I still surprised myself by giving thanks for the day.

We planted flowers. That was important. Our first insights of Hurd gained greater depth. Our intuitions found substance.

Hurd was excited as we unloaded flats and pots of hot house flowers from the old truck. The drab rattletrap looked like an inflated planter, a cartoon pottery from the five and ten. We graded out beds in front of a newly-constructed building.

"Think in lines. Make pictures of lines across. Across!" Hurd was intense. When the beds were as uniform as combed sand we broke pots and passed plants while he troweled the soil.

"Nature's line a curve is. The nest. The limb. The leaf, always in curves. See, like water falling. In back, tall plants. In front, petunia." His hands moved the soil making an absolute sculpture of flowers. Digging, planing, hammering to pack, smoothing, the plants arranged in fountains under the stubby fingers. They borrowed color from each other. They were green, red, yellow against the black earth. Hurd's face was a tense mask.

He pushed hard for three hours. When he finished he was exhausted, a man who had done a beautiful thing. The beds looked like some consummate portraiture of all gardens, tributes to color and life. I was filled with a realization when Hurd seemed to recollect himself and said apologetically, "I love these things to do."

Apologetic. The man had suffered the creative experience. I know it too well, have in the past exhausted myself in the tension, in the rising movement and roll of words. I have seen it in the passion of students and dedicated teachers. I have seen Pike sing with tears trailing eyes to broad nose to salt-tasting on his thick lips. And here, planting flowers, Hurd had been exalted.

"I love these things to do." I privately gave thanks. Why would a man not give thanks and look forward to the beginning of every day.

We were taken from climbing to meet the emergency of the spring planting season. There is so little time then. Every man and every truck is occupied with budding trees. Our first was a single tree in conjunction with other work.

"*Prunus serrulata*, double flower cherry. Is beautiful." Hurd walked in the half light of the company yard down a long row of balled trees until he found our tree. It was fourteen feet, a good size, and just beginning to crack out buds. We could not see that it was beautiful. It looked like an accumulation of sticks. Later, we understood. After planting we watched the tree. In three weeks it had a beauty so great that small boys attacked it with sticks because it hurt something in them. We scattered a pack of them one day when the sky was flawless and the grass in the courtyard was high enough to display the wind.

Hurd raised his hands. He moved his head. Then he approached the tree, head down and murmuring. He waved us away. While Pike went to the garage for our truck I watched him. He touched the tree, speaking softly, plucked a broken twig, tested the ball.

Gnome-like. Strange. In the beginning light, my mind alive with action, work, beauty and desire, I saw Hurd as someone alien, something legendary thrown up to life by the soil itself. He seemed bearer of a bizarre, particular, and perhaps useless knowledge that spoke the experience of many springs. He was married to someone. Was he in love? A mysterious man in a mysterious spring, so that later in the day, hearing the far away tap of high heels on a side-walk, I wanted to love a woman gently, with respect, and tell her of Hurd murmuring into a tree.

Pike returned with the truck and we loaded carefully. "The tree tight in the ball is. Do not break loose." It was heavy but we did not scrape bark with the small winch. After padding with burlap we drove to the job.

To plant a tree. Hard work, but so is setting fence posts. It is simple in mechanics. Dig wide, dig deep. Clear rocks and back-fill to make a cushion of soil. Center the tree perfectly and high to allow for settling. Tamp in enough soil to hold the position. Water. Fill halfway with soil and free the ball with knives. Spit in the hole and fill the rest of the way. Tamp and water in after forming the berm. Drive anchors with wire attached, cut hose and secure. In the East it takes an hour. In the West fifteen minutes because the trees are grown in cans and holes are augered. But trees blow down in the West.

"What?"

"Spit."

"Why?" Pike was puzzled.

"It is a custom." Hurd was being formal. We spit.

"Custom?"

"Old men sometimes make their fingers bleed." Hurd was absolutely shy and turned from us to avoid questions. He growled at the tree. Low-voiced. Commanding. "Black man, brown man, white man. Lucky. You . . . Grow."

We talked that night. Past our sleep.

"The German mind," Pike said. "Perfect mechanics. When he grades or plants, rigs; even the tools. They're packed in precise order on the truck at the end of day. Perfect mechanics with a superstition to contradict."

"The tree will grow." I was tired. The evening was restful with a fatigue that felt good. We had money now. We ate at restaurants and coffee houses instead of in the room.

"A romantic," Pike grinned.

"The word alien is in my mind. I feel it with him. I feel it in the trees."

"Trees know?" Pike leaned back in his chair, stretching full length, his smile half-serious, half-teasing.

"With the intelligence of any life, of adaptability. Not intelligence as we understand it."

Pike became serious. "I know. I'm dealing with a live thing, a living presence. That's it. You feel presence because of life." He was surprising himself.

"No good," I told him. "There are many forms of life. Poison ivy, amoebas."

"But that life does not weigh two or three tons and support your weight, your own life, indifferently."

"I'm not sure," I admitted.

"Neither am I."

We watched Hurd. We did not solve the romance of the trees. I have never solved that although I understand that there are fragments of general truth in the persuasion that causes arborists to speak to plants. We did solve other questions. The equation of Hurd balanced. A man's grief for another man and, by proxy, all men, pulsed in Pike's young music and became a familiar tune that found sympathy in the restlessness of many people.

We were working a line of small maples in full leaf. We were shinning. On my third tree I was stopped in the first crotch. The tree was suddenly filled with a flutter and crying that caused me to climb down. A robin feared for her nest. The tree had been structured at some previous time. The top could be lightened later. I walked down the row to the next tree in line. It was not until an hour before quitting time that we finished the maples and were ready to drop back some lilac. Hurd worked the first two to be sure we understood.

We began work. Hurd turned to the row of maples. He was making a decision. He picked up pole pruner and pole saw, then walked to the tree. In the frenzy of the bird's fluttering worry he pruned the tree. We watched. He worked rapidly, carefully. He took a secondary above the nest. It whipped the nest hard in falling.

"Why?" Pike said. "Now she'll leave."

When Hurd finished the nest seemed intact. The bird returned. The cover was gone. The tree was open to air and sunlight. It was thick enough to be a measure against scald but too thin to conceal a nest.

"Will she leave?" Pike asked.

"Maybe." He was surly. On our way back to the yard we did not talk much. The next morning Hurd was combative. When we arrived at the job we made a point of ignoring the tree. Hurd looked. He walked to the tree to find the nest abandoned. Then he walked back to us. "One thing understand. Sing. Talk. Good. But things must be done exact."

"Sure," Pike said, "I think I understand." The rest of the day passed in much work and little talk.

"Got it," Pike said that evening. "It makes me want to be drunk."

"You don't drink," I told him. We were lingering over coffee. Two girls at a near table pretended indifference to us. It was only pretense. My country raising hurt. They were white girls, perhaps intelligent and wonderful girls. They were in Harvard Square where things could be different, but I was not different and neither was Pike.

"The way Hurd was brought up. I'll bet that's it."

"I need a woman. Hard work is lonesome without being loved."

Pike looked at me. "I know. Listen, take a totalitarian regime."

"I'm going to California this fall."

"I'll go with you. Something will happen there."

"I don't mean a pick-up. I want to love somebody more than I love myself."

"Yes," Pike said, "easy and good without any mess about people watching. Bring flowers, make love, all of it."

"Nothing for free."

"Right. Now forget it until autumn because thinking about it hurts."

"Sure. What about Hurd?"

"He is a cripple," Pike said. "Get more coffee. I want to develop this."

I went for coffee. The girls looked expectant when I stood up.

"For us," Pike said, "it's occasionally a little rough." His expression was reflective, his usually smooth forehead glistened and held the trace of a wrinkle. "Not much, maybe. But we have more work than we'll ever get done and we lose half of each year on jobs. Still, fifty percent is better than many have."

"Eliot worked in a bank."

"Sure. London went to sea. What odds?" He smiled that slow smile that whips emotion into so many. "But real pain? Permanent damage? No. We have trouble, maybe, but no one has a patent on trouble. Permanent pain we don't have. Be glad."

"But Hurd?"

"Is injured. He is truly lost. Except for something occasional like the flowers he is only putting up with life, with the traffic, with this blown cotton smog."

"All right." I turned. The girls were leaving. I watched sadly because the one with dark hair, the shorter one who had slim ankles and high breasts also seemed sad. Imagination perhaps.

"What I mean," Pike also watched them leave, "is that Hurd is a sensitive man with a steel spine. Regulated. Modeled out of size and shape. Destroyed as an artist . . . wait." He saw my objection. "The art is there, the ability to form, the need for beauty. But he is overloaded with mechanics and the rules of order. He may not grow beyond discipline. He may not leave a nest untouched if it contradicts a rule. He may not express emotion beyond any rule."

"Some talent does that." As I began to protest I suspected that Pike was correct.

"The Nazis killed more men than those who laid down."

"You're making too much of this." He surprised me. His mind seemed to be straying some nebulous route that he was not defining.

"Not now." Pike's face was questioning. "He is our friend. In a way he is our mentor. We have learned no answers but we have learned his question . . . the one expression he has left."

"Which is?"

"The search. What's at the top of a tree?" Pike stood to leave. "He has patterned his life to greenery, wondering if there is understanding there. With his accent, with his iron spine, with his yearning for beauty he stands totally damned." He looked at me, unblinking and unembarrassed by emotion. His face was easy, but his eyes were a violence.

"I think of my father," he said quietly, "a man Hurd was taught to hate."

"He does not hate us."

"He does not hate at all. If there was hatred it's withered. It makes no sense in a world of vegetation."

"I must go to California soon."

Pike did not answer. We left, Pike breathing notes to himself as he often did. From them came the music which begins:

> The theme of a life that is nurtured in hate,
> Is the moan of a wind through the thorns,
> Of a tree dispossessed by its nature which waits,
> Thrusting limbs where no nest will be borne . . . .

Not strictly true, perhaps. A few birds build in honey locust and hawthorne, but very few. The song for a German was taken by liberal students to the ghetto with passion. It was to make Pike famous.

But that was later. That was after two years of San Francisco in commerce with the blue and golden west, with the heart-hurt-filling beauty of a city too various for an artist's good. Until September we worked with Hurd, our youth believing we could cut through or explode the past. It was then that Pike began taking his guitar to work.

Hurd worried about impropriety but allowed the guitar. There was no specific rule. Pike played for the rest of the summer. Once, on poor impulse, I read from Walden but the reading went poorly.

"In Germany in jail that man would be." The old face of Hurd distorted trying to follow the sense of the reading. Understanding caused his face to wrinkle with anger and alarm.

"Men must work. Always is the work. Cut here. Climb. Grade this. Twenty years it takes, old men say. Twenty years the rake to learn." Hurd was at least fifty. He spoke always of the old men. I imagined them to look like a steel engraving of God, a rendition of authority by Blake.

"Have you always worked with plants?" I closed the book.

"Yah. Yes. Once," Hurd grinned and his shyness was gone now, "Once, a dancer I would be."

"Hey," Pike breathed. "Hey, hey."

"What kind of dance?"

"Each kind. Every kind. Once I saw a show of tap dance."

"Why didn't you?"

"School."

His father had been caretaker of a large estate, a man imbued with antique mysticisms of peasantry as well as great practical knowledge. A man wise with soil. When Hurd was old enough the estate's owners sent him to school where he earned a degree in horticulture. He had learned it all, all that was known in those days of manures, soil, plants, grades, irrigation, drainage, erosion, grass, pruning, brickwork, grafting . . . all. We had not suspected his vast information.

"I want to learn," Pike said, "and there isn't much time. Teach me what you can."

"I teach you maybe wrong. Much has changed."

"I'll risk it." Pike's grin was eager. "A student I will be."

"So!"

We entered a quick apprenticeship. Hurd was demanding. He became enthusiastic as we were enthusiastic. Each day in the trees he repeated information. He tried to make clear why a thing was so. We learned disease of plants. We learned to distinguish grasses, blue, rye, fescue. Our notes were filled with formulae. Mine is before me now. "60 gal. puts 1 in. wtr. in 100 sq. ft. soil av."

Another education. A system of cause and reason given our love for life and for the work, between which we did not distinguish. For a time I felt near to solving the feeling of presence in the trees.

"What did you do," Pike asked one day, "when the war was on?" It was a question we dreaded to ask, feared to ask. We imagined that Hurd would react terribly. Yet, it had to be asked. We were learning from the man.

Hurd seemed unsurprised by the question. Perhaps his surprise was that we had waited so long. He looked at Pike, at Pike's hands. "In South Africa I raised rubber."

"South Africa? One of the big plantations?"

"Yes. Please do not ask me, Pike. Was good and bad. Like always."

And that is all we knew, all we know, although we conjectured with more imagination than knowledge.

In a way we were glad for the ending. Our admiration for each other, the feeling of our small group's integrity, was perfect. It is rarely that situations or lives have the chance to end on the highest tonal expression. Had we stayed some things might have become common, some thoughts too familiar. No, there is always a perfect time to leave and too often we wistfully out-stay that time.

On the last day of work we were sad. After work we did an unusual thing. We walked, commanding Hurd's presence, until we found a bar where we ordered beer. Partings are bad. The gestures are often worse. In this we succeeded because for a few moments we were wise.

"I will write at Christmas," Pike told him. "Once a year is best. Day to day is common."

"Is good."

"So will I," I told him. "Or when I finish the book or when big things happen."

"I wish . . . ."

"You must take this," Pike interrupted him. "We looked for some fine thing." He handed Hurd the book on Japanese gardens we had settled for after much search and argument. It had cost twenty-five dollars and we were glad.

From his pocket Hurd reached the hand pruners we had used that summer, the brass jaws cut deep by the case-hardened blades. They are a personal tool, even now mine would cause a familiar weight riding cased on my hip. He handed them to us. No ceremony. I dropped mine in my pocket feeling that in some way I had been awarded a degree.

"Famous you will be," he told us. "Singing and words. But I . . . ."

"You," Pike interrupted, "are the lucky one. How many men are allowed to spend all their lives making beauty?"

"I would drink to that," I said, "except I've finished my beer. It's time to go. Good-bye. Thank you."

In two days we bought an old car and went west. For a while Pike and I roomed together in San Francisco until my book was finished. I wrote a second. The second sold. Pike became famous, renowned in a way.

All sums. When I kept the appointment with Pike I had not seen him in six or seven months.

We met in North Beach at a sidewalk restaurant we could not have afforded when we came. I arrived first, took possession of a table and watched the activity.

The sun was high, casting short shadows of tall buildings which stood like structured edifices of cloud. The lighting was intense. It cast the shadows of signs lining Broadway before each of the clubs. Pictures before the clubs, women with naked breasts and bartered smiles, were a gilt-glittering flash of blue, red, gold; spangles contrasting to the dusty fabric heavily draping the windows. Automobiles paused for traffic lights, stopping, starting, the heated tires on the hot pavement announcing in brief screeches each individual passage toward a particular illusion. Ice was spun tinkling in glasses, the sound intermixed with the low hum of conversation. A woman's perfume lingered in the heat, swirled by the crowds of people walking past. At the curb a street tree drooped, the familiar signs of dry or unproductive soil. *Ficus retusa*, Laural Fig. A sturdy tree and likely to survive.

Pike came in view, black-shining in conservative business dress. He was above the press of the crowd, had always been for me, and now he moved without hesitation, unjostled in the hurrying throng.

"I'm glad," he said, taking my arm and sitting down, and I knew that he meant glad to see me. The tables were filling. A heavy man in yachting costume with a smooth-shaven face like rough beef stepped past us puffing. He drew a chair for a young woman who was almost formally dressed.

"I'm glad, too," I told Pike. "Glad to see you."

We ate and spoke of little. The stylistic changes in his new album. My next book.

"Let's walk," Pike said when lunch was finished.

We walked. Down Broadway and into Grant. The coffee houses and Italian restaurants were dim. The art shops, the gift shops, the junk shops were a tangle of foppery and disrepair, the whole a gesture to opera and the jingle-jangle poetics worn at ankle and wrist.

"I called," Pike said. "When I got your message I called Cambridge. His helper refused a tree. There were only two of them working. He died in a main branching at about forty feet. Heart."

"Tied in?"

"He always tied in. 'Hurt you can be at five feet. Always tie in.'"

"I remember. I would have climbed for him."

"To take the tree?"

"Yes, or to bring him down."

Pike stopped before a window. It was filled with artistic wares, photographs, pottery buttons on leather thongs, hand-woven belts.

"What would he have been?" I asked.

"A gardener. His father was a gardener."

"The man, I mean. What kind of man?"

Pike turned. There was a low sullenness behind his eyes, some hurt, some anger. "Do not allow this to fool you. Nothing that he did will last. Growth and death. The form changes, things seed, new growth wipes out old designs."

A group of office workers walked by, sophisticated women, their legs trim, their clothing and hair as manicured as their nails. They laughed as they walked. Beyond us a driver rolled a barrel of tap beer from his truck. There was a faint smell of flowered incense from within a store and overhead an airplane droned in the blue, shadow-making sky.

"But the planting was good."

"It was all good." Pike's face seemed wrong. "But it's not why we're here. Of course it was good. The design had form, branches were encouraged to take over and grow, direction was given the tree."

"I understand. Who watches trees?" A boy of about fifteen ran past whistling. He was chased by his younger sister who ran seriously and panted. Two fat men stood on the curb arguing in Italian. An ancient man in a buttoned overcoat moved slowly past and shivered in the sun.

"I'm not good, you know, not good like I was." Pike's face seemed to be studying fear. The eyes, again. The eyes. They were estranged from his voice. "Love," he said in a low voice, ". . . speak that and be responsible for license. The edge is off somehow. Even the believing is off. Off."

"I know," I stumbled. "There's a bad importance in me that doesn't deny the applause."

"Yes," he said quickly. He was startled. "Yes," he repeated much more slowly. "Well, perhaps that's why we're here." The crowds jostled past, currents traveling the safe sidewalks enclosing the asphalted street. Pike spoke carefully, as if into the crowd.

"Diluted. Yet, we must say a word, bring something to bear that we will understand. It is more important than ever that we try to understand . . . the song, but that is paid for by violence, misunderstanding, self-pity."

"I would have lowered him very gently." My voice seemed too loud.

Pike started. He paused. "Then let that be the word." He clasped my arm with his strong hand, then turned and walked away quickly. I watched his broad shoulders, broadened more by the suit. I watched the thick negro hair shining in the sun. For a moment I turned away, feeling a reflection of my own longing, and turning, saw a dusty reflection of myself in the glare of the store window. I had tears and no tears, my breath laboring with the recollected feeling of youth. It passed. I returned my gaze to to scan the street. It was possible to distinguish Pike for nearly a block before he disappeared into the crowds that pooled before stop lights and eddied between crosswalks; that whispered, spoke, chattered, that murmured and questioned, the thronging sounds like a troubled current washing through valleys toward a vast and distant sea.